SPECIAL MESSAGE TO READERS

This book is published under the auspices of
THE ULVERSCROFT FOUNDATION
(registered charity No. 264873 UK)

Established in 1972 to provide funds for
research, diagnosis and treatment of eye diseases.
Examples of contributions made are: —

A new Children's Assessment Unit at
Moorfield's Hospital, London.
•
Twin operating theatres at the
Western Ophthalmic Hospital, London.
•
A Chair of Ophthalmology at the
University of Leicester.
•
The establishment of a Royal Australian College
of Ophthalmologists "Fellowship".

You can help further the work of the Foundation
by making a donation or leaving a legacy. Every
contribution, no matter how small, is received
with gratitude. Please write for details to:

**THE ULVERSCROFT FOUNDATION,
The Green, Bradgate Road, Anstey,
Leicester LE7 7FU, England.
Telephone: (0116) 236 4325**

**In Australia write to:
THE ULVERSCROFT FOUNDATION,
c/o The Royal Australian College of
Ophthalmologists,
27, Commonwealth Street, Sydney,
N.S.W. 2010.**

THE SILVER TOMBSTONE

When Johnny Fletcher and Sam Cragg's jalopy runs out of petrol, a Samaritan by the name of Joe Cotter pushes them to a motel and demands twenty dollars. Early the next morning, they siphon petrol from Cotter's convertible and make a hasty exit. However, they quickly dump their car when they discover a dead body sprawled in the back seat. They hitch a lift to Los Angeles, where a silver nugget comes hurtling through their hotel window. Is there a connection between this and the dead body?

FRANK GRUBER

THE SILVER TOMBSTONE

Complete and Unabridged

LINFORD
Leicester

First published in the
United States of America

First Linford Edition
published July 1995

British Library CIP Data

Gruber, Frank
  The Silver Tombstone.—Large print ed.—
  Linford mystery library
  I. Title II. Series
  823.912 [F]

  ISBN 0–7089–7730–8

Published by
F. A. Thorpe (Publishing) Ltd.
Anstey, Leicestershire
Set by Words & Graphics Ltd.
Anstey, Leicestershire
Printed and bound in Great Britain by
T. J. Press (Padstow) Ltd., Padstow, Cornwall

This book is printed on acid-free paper

1

ONCE you cross El Cajon Pass you can coast for a number of miles, but eventually you hit a flat stretch of road and then your car stops. From this point you can see the lights of San Bernardino, but you are still quite a few miles away — on a dark, lonely road.

"Well," said Johnny Fletcher, applying the emergency brake, "so much for your stars."

Big Sam Cragg winced. "What've the stars got to do with us running out of gas?"

"You tell *me*. The stars told you to come out to California. And here we are, right in the middle of it — in the middle of the night."

"That isn't fair, Johnny," Sam Cragg protested. "My horoscope said that conditions were favorable for making

1

a long journey . . . "

"And we made it — all the way across the country."

"Last winter we went to Florida," Sam retorted. "Because you wanted to play the horses. And what happened to us in Florida? It can't be any worse here, unless . . . "

"Unless what?"

"Unless you get stubborn and refuse to work."

Johnny Fletcher inhaled heavily. "I'll do my best, Sam. I promise."

"That's good enough for me!" Sam cried. "I know you don't believe in astrology, but I do — and I made another horoscope only this morning and it said even more positively that things were going to break for me."

"I'm glad to hear that," Johnny said with heavy irony. "If your luck is going to be so good suppose you stop this car that's coming."

Sam turned and looked at the approaching headlights. "Well, I'll try." He scrambled out of the car and ran around to the roadside. Johnny leaned back in the driver's seat, grinning cynically.

The car was coming swiftly. Sam leaned out and gave the hitchhiker's signal.

Brakes screeched and the car came to a halt beside Sam. It was a convertible with the top down and contained a single occupant, a man wearing the insignia of the Southwest — a two-gallon hat.

"What's the trouble, folks?" the driver asked cheerfully.

"Out of gas," Johnny said, making a quick recovery from his astonishment. "Wonder if you can give us a lift to the next town?"

"San Bernardino? It's fourteen miles. How would you get back with the gas?"

"We wouldn't — tonight."

"Oh, but you don't want to leave your car here all night. Why don't you let me push it?"

"You'd do that, Mister?" Sam Cragg cried.

"Why not?"

"I don't believe it," Johnny said, bluntly.

"Don't believe what?" the Samaritan asked.

"This California good neighbor stuff. I read about it in a book once, but I didn't believe it."

"Well, I don't know about California," said the man in the convertible. "You see, I'm from Arizona."

"That's different!" Johnny cried. He signalled to Sam and the big man hurried around to the other side of the car and climbed in.

The convertible backed away, then moved forward until its bumpers touched the rear bumpers of Sam and Johnny's jalopy. Johnny shifted into neutral and the powerful car behind gave the flivver a nudge that started it rolling. The driver was good — probably from much practice at this sort of thing. He kept the two cars touching. Only one or twice did he really bump the jalopy very hard.

4

The two cars rolled along at around thirty miles an hour and soon the lights of San Bernardino came closer. Finally the highway became a street lined on both sides with motels, each with its own brilliant blue and red neon sign.

"Say when!" yelled the driver of the pushing car.

Johnny turned. "This tourist camp's swell."

The Samaritan completed his good deed by pushing the jalopy into the court of the hotel. Johnny and Sam climbed out of their car and walked back.

"Mister," said Johnny. "That was doggone swell."

The driver grinned and climbed out of his car. "Oh, it wasn't anything really. A man's got to make a dollar whenever he can, you know."

A warning bell rang in Johnny's brain. He looked at the other man and made note of the fact that he was over six feet in height and tipped the beam at better than two hundred.

"Let's see," the big man continued. "Fourteen miles, say a dollar a mile . . . and my bumper's scratched pretty badly . . . mmm . . . about six or seven dollars' worth. Let's call the whole thing twenty dollars . . ."

Sam Cragg gasped. "Jeez!"

Johnny Fletcher nodded thoughtfully. "All right, let's *call* it twenty dollars."

"Fine!"

The big man grinned at Johnny and Johnny grinned back. Sam Cragg looked away.

"If you don't mind," said the not-so-good Samaritan. "It's after midnight and *I'd* like to get a little sleep."

The office door of the motel opened and a yawning man in a bathrobe came out. "Nice room, gents?" he asked.

"Yeah, sure," said Johnny.

"D'ya mind, fellows?" the big man said.

Johnny suddenly held out his hand. "You have my thanks, old man. Your kindness has touched my heart and if you will give me your name and home address . . . "

He broke off as the big man took his hand.

"Yow!" yelled Johnny and went down to his knees.

The man with the two-gallon hat chuckled and released Johnny's hand. "See what I mean?"

Johnny got up, trembling. His right hand was completely numb. Sam Cragg stepped forward, his eyes flashing from the light of a red neon sign.

"*I'd* like to shake your hand, Mister," he said in the same tone the devil uses when he tempts a poor victim.

"Why not?" the big man asked and took Sam's hand.

. . . Which is a good time to tell you about Sam Cragg. He is five feet eight inches tall and weighs two hundred and twenty pounds. Those two hundred and twenty pounds are bone and muscle and steel, hardened with a little tungsten. Sam tears New York and Chicago phone directories in half with his bare hands.

His hand gripped that of the big Arizonian . . . and Sam got the surprise his life. So did the other fellow.

Sam exerted pressure on his grip. So did the other man.

"I got two vacant rooms," the sleepy motel man said.

"What about the twenty?" the bad Samaritan gasped to Sam.

"The hell with you," Sam panted. "I can hang on all night."

Johnny peered into Sam's face — and whistled softly. Sam was taking it.

"Kinda silly, isn't this?" the big stranger grunted, putting on more pressure.

"Ain't it?" Sam gritted, calling on his reserve.

Johnny stepped forward. "Shall I hit him with a brick, Sam?"

"I wouldn't if I were you," the big man warned.

"I can hold him," Sam grunted.

"I doubt it." The big man's breath came heavily. "What's your name?"

"Sam Cragg. What's yours?"

"Joe Cotter."

"I'm Johnny Fletcher," offered the owner of that name "In case you're interested."

"I'm not," said Joe Cotter. "But this is going to cost you fellows more money. I'm raising the price to twenty-five."

Johnny turned to the bored motel man. "Show me your cabins. I think the boys want to be alone and play awhile."

The motel man looked sourly at Sam and Joe Cotter. "What're they holdin' hands for?"

"Ignore them," Johnny suggested.

Joe Cotter suddenly jerks his hand out of Sam Cragg's grip. He stepped quickly to the side of Johnny's jalopy and whisked out the ignition key.

"The hell with that stuff. I'll take this instead."

"Give me that key," Sam snarled.

Joe Cotter sighed wearily. "Look, Sam Cragg, you aren't a bad guy, but

I'm tired and sleepy. I'll go a couple of rounds with you if you insist but why not wait until morning? We'll both feel more like it."

"That sounds fair, Sam," Johnny said.

Sam hesitated. Then he finally growled, "All right, but give me the key."

"I'll keep it," Joe said. "Just in case you get the idea of running out during the night."

"I'm not afraid of you," Sam began.

"Let him have the key," Johnny cried. "I'm tired and I want to go to bed." He went off after the motel man.

The vacant rooms turned out to be side by side. The motel man led Johnny and Sam into the first. It was a nicely furnished room with a double bed.

"Three dollars," said the motel man.

Johnny yawned. "Okay, we'll take it."

"In advance!"

10

Johnny groaned. "Am I going to have trouble with *you*, now? We'll pay you in the morning . . . "

"The rules are . . . "

"I know, I know. But our car's outside. Sit in it all night if you're afraid we're going to run away with it."

"But — "

Johnny took the man's arm, led him firmly to the door and pushed him out. Then he closed the door and bolted it. After which he turned to Sam Cragg.

"You and your astrology!"

"I'll lick him in the morning," Sam muttered.

"Stay up all night and train for him," Johnny snarled. "Me — I'm going to get a good night's sleep."

Next door a woman screamed.

"Johnny!" Sam cried. "Did you hear that?"

"I'm not deaf. It's probably just someone being murdered. But I'm damned if I care!"

He threw himself upon the bed. Sam stared at him a moment, looked worriedly at the wall, then finally shrugged and moved to the bed.

Johnny Fletcher was already asleep.

2

IT was still dark when Johnny Fletcher opened his eyes. For a moment he lay still. Then the events of the evening before rushed back into his mind and he sat up. He reached out and shook Sam Cragg.

"Up, Sam!"

Sam Cragg groaned and stirred. "Whatsamatter?" he mumbled. "It ain't morning yet."

"It will be in a little while. We've got to get moving."

"Why?"

"Because we haven't got any gas," Johnny snapped. "And no ignition key."

The bed creaked and Sam Cragg sat up. "Oh!" he grunted. "It comes back now."

Johnny climbed out of bed and walked to the window. Brushing aside the curtain he looked out. "Dawn's breaking. Come on."

Not having undressed the night before their preparations for departure were simple. They merely walked out the door.

Outside the sky was greying. A light was on in the office building, but all the cabins were still dark. Shivering in the cool morning air, Johnny and Sam went to the old jalopy. From the glove compartment Johnny took three objects: a piece of wire, a length of rubber tubing and a canvas sack of the kind used for water by desert travelers. He handed the last two objects to Sam.

Sam scowled. "You know I don't like this stuff, Johnny."

"I don't like it, either, but we have between us the sum of sixty-five cents, which may or may not buy us enough gas to get to Los Angeles."

Sam sighed. "All right, all right." He moved off toward a convertible parked nearby — Joe Cotter's car.

While he busied himself about the gas tank, Johnny performed his own little job, which consisted of attaching the piece of wire to the starter, so that a spark would jump from the ignition-sans ignition key.

Sam returned with a canvas sack full of gasoline and poured it into the gas tank of the jalopy. "Better get another," Johnny suggested. "Seeing it's Joe's car."

Two minutes later with Sam beside him, Johnny stepped on the starter. The motor caught instantly and they started out of the motel yard. As they passed the office a man came out and called to them, but Johnny pretended not to hear.

Johnny drove quickly through San Bernardino. With the lights of the city behind them he began chuckling. Sam looked at him. "What's so funny?"

"I'd like to see that cowboy's face when he finds our car missing."

"I'd just as soon have stayed there and had it out with him," Sam said.

"The big palooka!"

He hunched down lower in his seat, scowling. After a moment he glanced surreptitiously at Johnny and drew a booklet from his pocket. Johnny shot a quick sideward glance and saw the title of the book: "Astrology In 12 Easy Lessons," he read aloud. "Here we go again."

"Go ahead, laugh," Sam said. "But I've got a funny feeling — as if something's about to happen." He turned the page. "Let's see — today's the ninth. Yeah, Uranus is rising in Jupiter. Sons of Aquarius should be very careful all day, lest ill fortune befall them . . . "

"That was yesterday," Johnny interrupted. "Everything's in reverse. You predicted good luck yesterday and we had bad. Today . . . "

Sam Cragg, turning his head casually, jerked and cried out in horror.

Johnny's head swiveled, and the car careened wildly across the road. He regained control before it went into the ditch, brought it over to the right side and braked it. Then he looked into the tonneau of the flivver.

A man was sprawled there — his legs on the floor, the upper part of the body on the seat. The handle of a knife protruded from his back.

"He's dead!" Sam gasped. Then his eyes widened. "Uranus rising in Jupiter. The sons of Aquarius . . . "

"Ah, hell," Johnny snarled. "The woman who screamed next door during the night — "

"A woman couldn't have dragged this baby out and lifted him into the car," Sam mumbled, shaking his head.

"There's a car coming," Johnny exclaimed. He whirled and stepped on the starter. Fortunately he had not removed the wire and the motor caught. He shifted into second, stepped on the accelerator and moved into high.

"He's coming pretty fast," Sam cried.

Fifty feet ahead, a narrow paved road

cut the main highway. Johnny turned into it.

"He's gone past," Sam reported.

Johnny nodded. Suddenly he drove the car off the pavement, over a shallow ditch into an orange grove. Twenty feet from the road he stopped the car.

"End of the line," he said, shortly.

"You gonna dump him here?"

"No — I'm going to leave the car here."

"Why not just the body?"

"We can't take a chance. They'll know us by the car . . . "

"But they'll check up on the license plates."

"Let them. They'll find that a Mort Murray of New York City bought the plates. I never bothered to have the registration changed when I bought the heap from Mort . . . Mort'll cover up for us. He'll say the car was stolen from him and since it had no value he didn't report it. Which is almost true."

"The car isn't that bad. It brought us all the way across the country."

"Which was the eighth miracle of the world . . . Better take the books. We'll need a stake."

Sam hesitated then reached gingerly into the rear of the car, almost under the lower half of the torso and brought out a large, heavy carton, tied with a heavy cord.

Johnny took one last look at the car, then shook his head and started for the road. A few minutes later they were back on the main highway.

A car came along and Johnny used his thumb The driver grinned derisively as he sped past.

"Maybe it's just as well we don't get any more lifts," Johnny said philosophically.

Sam Cragg was of a different opinion. "Everybody can't be like that cowboy. It's forty-some miles to L.A. You don't think I can walk that far, do you?"

"In one day? It's pretty stiff. But we ought to make it by tomorrow . . . Unless . . . what's that ahead, Sam?"

"Car with a flat tire. And . . . yeah, I see what you mean . . . "

A hundred feet ahead a yellow convertible was parked at the side of the road. The left rear tire was flat. Surveying it was a girl in a yellow suit that almost matched the color of the car. As they approached Johnny saw that the girl was in her early twenties. She was tall and slender . . . yet filled out in the right places. Johnny liked her very much. Beside him Sam Cragg whistled softly.

The car had New York license plates.

"Hello," Johnny greeted the girl. "Shall we change your tire?"

"Why?" the girl asked.

"Because it's flat . . . "

"Oh, is it? How observing."

Johnny grinned. "Right from Times Square!"

"Times Square?"

"Us, too." Johnny kicked the flat tire. "Sam, take this off."

"Oh, don't bother," said the girl. "Someone will come along . . . "

"Someone *has* come along." Johnny walked around to the far side of the car and, leaning over, reached into the glove compartment for the driver's registration card. "Helen Walker," he read. "How do you do? I'm Johnny Fletcher and my friend here is Sam Cragg. Strange — three people from Times Square meeting out here in California."

"There must be at least fifty thousand people from New York in California," said the girl. "And about a half million from Iowa."

"Yes, but Iowans don't stick together like New Yorkers." Johnny nodded toward Sam, laboring with the spare tire. "One New Yorker always does a good turn for another . . . when they meet away from home . . . "

The girl looked at Johnny, somewhat puzzled. "We're going to L.A.," he said, significantly.

She got it, then. Although she made no comment. Sam Cragg took out the jack from under the car and returned

21

it to the luggage compartment, along with the flat tire. He let the door slam down and dusted his hands.

The girl opened the car door. "I'm sorry," she said, "but I never give rides to hitchhikers. It isn't safe."

Johnny blinked. "Hitchhikers!"

The girl nodded to Sam Cragg. "Thank you for changing the tire." She got into the car.

"Wait a minute," cried Johnny. "You've forgotten something!"

Helen Walker, turned and looked inquiringly at him.

"Our charge for changing tires is one dollar," Johnny said, tightly.

She looked at him steadily for a moment, then opened her purse. "Of course. Here's a dollar . . . and a quarter for yourself, my good man."

Johnny took the money. The girl started the car and it jerked away.

Johnny stood looking after it. Sam Cragg came up beside him. "Jeez, Johnny," he said. "That was pretty raw."

"And what about her? 'I never give rides to hitchhikers.'" He muttered something under his breath. "At least we can ride in a bus now."

Sam brightened a little. "Yeah, I wasn't so keen on hanging around this neighborhood."

3

SHORTLY after eleven o'clock that morning Johnny Fletcher and Sam Cragg alighted from a bus on Hollywood Boulevard. Johnny looked up and down the street.

"If you ask me it looks just like Topeka, Kansas. Well — what does your astral guide tell you?"

"I'm afraid to look in the book. Besides — I'm hungry. Why don't we go to work?"

"Where?"

"You never bothered about that before." Sam glanced uneasily at his friend. "You're not losing your grip, are you?"

"Me?" Johnny laughed. "There isn't a cop in sight, is there?"

"I don't see any. But you can't go to work right here on the corner . . . "

"You challenged me, Sam." Johnny

shook his head in mock injury. "Get ready!"

Sam peeled off his coat and dropped it to the sidewalk. He removed the rope from about the carton.

"Okay!"

Johnny stepped out to the edge of the sidewalk, waved his arms and began talking. He had an astonishing voice for so lean a man. It boomed across the street, was hurled back by the buildings on the other side and arrested the attention of everyone within the block.

"Gentlemen!" he thundered. "And ladies, too. Step closer, please. We're going to show you one of the most amazing exhibitions of strength it has ever been your privilege to witness. My friend here, Young Samson, is known throughout this country and Europe as the perfect specimen of physical manhood."

He pointed at Sam who was stripping off his shirt. He had a web belt in one hand. "Look at his rippling muscles, his wonderful physique. Have you ever seen the likes, anywhere — at any time . . . "

He lowered his voice to a confidential bellow. "Young Samson is undoubtedly the strongest man that has ever appeared in this town — in the great state of California. He has consented to exhibit himself because I personally asked him to do so, for a reason you'll learn in a moment . . . What, gentlemen? Some of you are skeptical? You don't think he's as strong as I say? You don't think he's as strong as I say? Just a minute, before we go any further. We'll prove it. Samson!"

Johnny took the web belt from Sam's hand, put it about Sam's chest and buckled it. Then he turned back to his audience, now numbering some hundred odd, about half men and the rest women and children.

"Gentlemen, particularly those of you who have seen strong men — you know that one of these belts is strong enough to lift a mule. Have any of you ever seen a man break one? No, of course you haven't. Well . . . *Samson!*"

Sam Cragg, alias Young Samson, let the air out of his lungs. Then he clenched his fists and slowly drew a deep breath. His chest expanded . . . until the strong belt cut into his skin and flesh . . .

Then there was a loud 'pop' and the belt flew away from Sam Cragg. Johnny scooped it up and held it aloft. "Look closely, gentlemen! Note that it didn't break at the buckle — but in the exact center. And notice, too, that it wasn't cut or weakened in any manner . . . Look!"

Johnny stooped and brought out a length of chain from the carton. He fumbled it, dropping it to the pavement, where it made a resounding clank. He picked it up again.

"Gentlemen!" he roared. "I see your expression of astonishment. I can read your minds. You're thinking — surely he isn't going to break that chain. Good heavens, no! A horse couldn't break it . . . "

He ran the chain swiftly about Sam's chest, brought it together in front and linked it securely. Then he stepped away.

"I'm joking, of course," he informed the crowd. "No human being could break such a chain. But . . . " He dropped his voice suddenly to a hush that penetrated to the edge of the large audience. Then he took a deep breath and roared. "But suppose he *did* break that chain! What an amazing, tremendous feat of strength that would be. What a miracle! What? . . . You people want to see a miracle performed? You *want* to see Young Samson break the chain? You think he might, just barely *MIGHT* be able to do it?"

He shook his head sadly, looked at Sam Cragg and leaned his head toward his friend. Sam mumbled something. An expression of amazement leaped into Johnny's eyes.

"He says he can do it!" he cried out. "He's going to try. And I'm going to let him. Why? Because I know Young

28

Samson better than any living human. I know that he is the strongest man in the entire country! How do I know that? Why . . . ? Because I made him that!"

He paused dramatically for effect, then let his voice roll out — fuller and louder than before. "You think I'm crazy? Well, how about it, Samson? Tell them — did I make you as strong as you are? Weren't you a mere weakling when you first came to me? Didn't you weigh a hundred and thirty pounds? Go ahead . . . tell them!"

Sam Cragg bobbed his head. "Yah!"

Johnny threw up his hands. "You see, he admits it. He gives me the sole credit for his amazing strength. How did I do it? Ah, my friends, that is the secret. I'm going to tell you only that several years ago, I, too, was a weakling. I was consumptive — weighed ninety-five pounds. The doctors gave me three months to live. I was desperate. I didn't want to die.

I wanted to be well and strong, like other men. I wanted the respect of my fellow men — women. For who loves a weakling? . . . Well, look at me now. I'm not exactly a weakling although not nearly the specimen that Sa — Young Samson is. I don't want to be. But I do want to impart my knowledge to others — the things I discovered back there in those black days. The secret of life, you might call it. This secret, my friends, I cannot tell you in public — except that it was exercise. Oh — don't wince, my friends. It's not as bad as all that. For these exercises are simple — so simple that anyone can perform them without strain. And so marvelous that in a week you will be a new man . . . in two weeks you will be able to break belts like my friend did a moment ago . . . In a month . . . LOOK!"

Sam Cragg suddenly went into a crouch. Clenching his fists he came up slowly, his chest expanding, the chain cutting into his chest . . .

The chain broke. It flew away from

Sam Cragg, and almost struck a man six feet away.

A murmur of awe ran through the audience. It was punctuated by Johnny Fletcher's scream. "He did it! He broke the chain that no human being could break — except Young Samson!" He stooped, whipped open the carton and took out a book.

"Here it is, folks! The book that contains the secrets of health, vitality, strength . . . the same simple rules and exercises that made Young Samson the strongest man in this country — in the whole world. They're all in here, simplified, condensed, abbreviated. I'm going to let you have these books now — not for twenty-five dollars each, not even twenty and God knows that would be little enough to pay for such secrets. No, friends, it's my duty to make these books available to everyone and that's why I'm going to practically give them away, asking just enough to pay for the printing and binding — a measly, paltry insignificant two dollars and ninety-five cents . . . "

"How much?" asked a voice.

Joe Cotter, the strong man from San Bernardino, pushed through the crowd. Johnny took one look at him and faltered. "T-two, n-ninety . . . five . . . "

"Cheap," said Joe Cotter. He stopped and picked up the chain with the broken link. With a quick movement he raised his knee and placing the chain under the knee gave a mighty jerk. The chain broke in two!

For a moment there was a dead silence. Then someone laughed. The crowd took it up and in a moment Sam and Johnny were in the midst of a jeering, roaring crowd. At the same time Sam saw a blue uniform come running across the street. He grabbed up his coat and shirt, the carton of books and ducked into the closest store. Johnny followed, crowding a thin anemic-looking man.

The man closed the door behind Johnny. "The cop won't come in here," he assured Johnny.

Johnny nodded. "Thanks, old man." He looked around and saw that they were in a luggage store. Sam began putting on his shirt. "I'll murder that Joe Cotter," he muttered.

"Next time we see him, I'll *let* you murder him," Johnny replied.

The little man was watching Sam closely. "You certainly got a good build, mister." He turned to Johnny. "I saw your act. I, uh, wonder, if you'd mind selling me one of your books?"

Johnny blinked. "Are you kidding?"

"Not at all. Your friend's pretty strong. 'Course that other guy was strong, too, but I imagine he's naturally that way. Young Samson used to be like, I, ha, am now."

Johnny reached out and clapped the little man on the shoulder.

"Friend, this is your lucky day!"

The little man backed away suddenly. "Course, you understand I'm a merchant myself. I expect you to sell me the

33

book, wholesale . . . say about forty per cent off."

Johnny grinned hugely. "Mister, I'll do better than that. I'll *swap*." He looked around the store. "What I need is a nice, expensive-looking suitcase — something like that genuine imitation leather one right there."

"Oh, but that bag's eight ninety-five . . ."

"Retail," said Johnny.

Five minutes later the deal was concluded — an even swap of two volumes of *Every Man A Samson* for the suitcase. Johnny emptied the remaining books into the suitcase and handed it to Sam.

When they reached the street, Sam Cragg exploded. "What was the good of that? The suitcase doesn't make us any better off. The box was good enough to carry the books . . ."

"Ah, but could you check into a hotel with just a paper carton?"

Sam was startled. "You mean you're going to clip a hotel again?"

"I don't like that word 'clip,' Sam. I ask you — can a man walk the street all night and be expected to go out and earn a living the next day? Is it my fault that hotels are owned by soulless corporations who don't think an honest man has the right to sleep in a bed? Just because they have a silly rule about making a man pay in advance if he hasn't got luggage is no reason why *I* should be deprived of my rights as a citizen."

Sam groaned and pointed ahead. "Is that the hotel we're going to — the Fremont?"

"It looks like a nice place."

"They always are. We couldn't clip a nice, small hotel. No, we've got to pick the biggest and most expensive ones."

"Here's the proposition," Johnny chuckled. "We can't both check in with a single piece of luggage, so one of us will have to rent the room and the other come for a visit. I'll toss you for it."

"No-no," Sam said hastily. "You get the room."

Johnny nodded and taking the suitcase went ahead of Sam. At the last moment his nerve failed him a little and he went around the corner to the side entrance in order to duck the doorman. A bellboy grabbed him just inside the lobby, however.

Johnny surrendered the suitcase and bore down upon the desk.

"What've you got in a nice room and bath?" he asked the clerk.

"I can give you something for four, five or six." The clerk hesitated a moment. "Or a lovely sitting room and bedroom for only ten dollars."

"Has the bedroom got a bed big enough for a man to stretch out in?"

"Just the biggest bed in California, that's all."

"Good! I'll take it."

The clerk tapped a bell. "Front!"

The bellboy who had grabbed Johnny's suitcase sprang forward. The clerk handed him a key. "Show Mr.

Fletcher to Suite 1032."

"1032," Johnny said, loudly. "Is that in front?"

"Oh yes — and very quiet."

Johnny followed the bellboy toward the elevators, winking at Sam Cragg, sitting in a leather chair.

The suite was a very nice one, containing a pull-down bed in the sitting room, in addition to the double bed in the bedroom. The bellboy fussed around the bathroom and opened and closed windows. Finally, when he could stall no longer he stepped up to Johnny and looked him straight in the eye. "Will that be all . . . *sir?*"

Johnny reached into a pocket. "Have you got change for a twenty?"

"Of course," said the bellboy. "I always carry change for a twenty."

"Oh," said Johnny. "Then a quarter wouldn't mean very much to you."

"It wouldn't — but I'll take it."

Johnny shook his head. "My boy, you're a cynic. You know all the answers — "

"And most of the routines. You're figuring on talking me out of the tip. Okay. But when you want some service around here don't ask for Bellboy Number Three. Now, go and squawk to the manager . . . and I'll tell him you've got a two-buck suitcase loaded with bricks. I'd tell him anyway, only I'm sore at him right now."

"Tsk, tsk," said Johnny. "And to think that a boy like you probably had a mother."

"I had a wife, too. I pay her thirty bucks a week alimony." The boy made a moist raucous sound with his mouth and departed. A moment later Sam Cragg came in. He glanced about the suite.

"Might as well be hung for a sheep as a lamb."

"Why not?"

Knuckles massaged the door. Johnny opened it and looked at a huge, muscle-bound man of about forty.

"I'm the house officer," the man said. "I just wanted to see if everything was okay." His eyes focused on the single suitcase.

"Everything's fine," Johnny said. "Only I've been wondering where a man could place a bet on a horse in this town. A friend of mine's got an awfully good one running today at Belmont . . . "

"What's his name?"

"The horse or my friend?"

"The horse."

"Mr. Copperman."

"Mr. Copperman?" The house detective frowned. "What price is he quoted at?"

"Twelve to one. My pal's been holding him back. He'll win in a walk."

"Is that a fact? Well, they're kinda tough in this town these days, but I'll tell you what . . . I mean, if you really want to put down a bet, why, I might . . . "

Johnny winked. "I'm going to run over to the bank. Suppose I look you up in about a half hour?"

"Fine, Mr., uh . . . ?"

"Fletcher. And you?"

"Tim O'Hanlon."

Johnny nodded and closed the door gently on the detective. He turned to Sam, a glint in his eye. "That damn bellboy! I see where I'm going to have to stay sharp around here."

"I hope you stay sharp long enough to unload those books and get us a stake," Sam Cragg said.

"A steak?" Johnny exclaimed. "With French fried potatoes? Why not?" He started quickly across the room, in the direction of the telephone. As he passed the table his leg brushed against the leg. A rough splinter caught at the cloth; there was a 'r-rip' and Johnny cried out in consternation.

"Goddamit, no!"

But there was a seven-inch rip in his trousers, from thigh to knee. Johnny dropped into a chair and stared at the rip like a man in great agony.

Sam Cragg whistled. "Gosh, what a rip."

"And us with a dollar forty-five between us!" Johnny wailed.

"Maybe we can borrow a needle and thread from the housekeeper," Sam suggested.

"The stitching will show." Johnny shook his head in despair. "How can I keep up a front with a pair of pants like this? I've got to get a new suit."

Sam quailed suddenly as if someone had struck him an invisible blow. "Johnny, you're not going to . . . "

Johnny got up heavily. "I don't know," he said, shaking his head. "We're strangers here; if this were New York I might be able to figure out something. But here in Los . . . " He stopped, his eyes fixed on something that he saw through the window.

Sam moved up quickly beside Johnny. He looked out of the window, but for a moment could not determine what Johnny was staring at so fixedly. Then he saw and exclaimed.

"No, Johnny, no . . . "

"California Credit Clothiers," Johnny

read. "'Buy Clothes the Modern Way. E – Z Terms.'"

"It won't work," Sam said. "You've got to have a down payment."

"Who says so?"

Johnny strode quickly to the bureau across the room and jerked open the top drawer. He exclaimed in satisfaction as he found a cushion containing several pins. Stooping, he pinned together the rip in his trousers, as best he could. It covered the bare flesh of his leg, but that was about all.

"Now, let me see," he mused aloud. "I'll only have one chance, so it's got to be done right. I'll need your help . . . "

"I couldn't carry it off," Sam protested. "They'd know I was gypping them . . . "

"Who said anything about gypping?" Johnny demanded innocently. "They're offering to sell on credit and that's all I want. I'll pay them for their suit . . . when I get some money."

"An outfit like that knows the routines . . . "

"So do I. And some maybe that they haven't heard. It's all in the way it's done. But I think you're right, you'd give the show away. Better keep your mouth shut. But back up my play."

"I'll go with you," said Sam, "but if they hear my knees knocking, I can't help it."

They left the suite and rode down to the lobby. There Johnny popped into the phone booth a moment. When he stepped out Sam looked at him, puzzled.

"What'd you do that for?"

"Quiet," admonished Johnny. "I'm trying to remember . . ."

Out on the street, he muttered half aloud . . . "Hillcrest 1251, Hillcrest 1251 . . ."

He turned east on Hollywood Boulevard. Sam looked at him in surprise then shrugged.

4

A BLOCK and a half down the boulevard Johnny exclaimed in satisfaction. "I knew there'd be one nearby." He nodded to a small shop, over which was a sign: *Job Printing.*

He turned in, Sam at his heels.

A man stopped a small Kelly job press and wiped his hands on his short printer's apron. "What can I do for you, gents?"

"Like to get some printing done," Johnny said. "Opening an office here on the Coast and need some stationery."

The printer brightened. "That's fine, Mister. Some letterheads and envelopes, maybe?"

Johnny nodded. "Can you give me a price on some good twenty-pound letterheads in two colors — about ten thousand quantity, and envelopes to match."

"Why, yes," said the printer. He got samples out of his display case. "Here's a nice Hammermill Bond. I can print you up a very neat two-color letterhead on this stuff, for only seven-fifty a thousand — in ten thousand quantity. And envelopes — Number Ten — to match, at only six-fifty a thousand."

"Good. And how about some business cards, for our salesmen. Something like this . . . " Johnny picked up a pencil and wrote on a sheet of paper:

Transcontinental Terra Cotta
Tile Corporation
8368 Sunset Blvd.
Hollywood, California.
Hillcrest 1251   Sam C. Cragg,
          Pacific Coast Manager

"Better figure on five thousand of these cards, but in five lots, with the names of the salesmen changed — one thousand for each salesman."

The printer nodded enthusiastically

and did some quick calculation. "Four-fifty a thousand," he concluded.

Johnny pursed up his lips. "Seventy-five dollars for letterheads, sixty-five for envelopes and twenty-two fifty for cards . . . mmm, a total of one hundred sixty-two dollars and fifty cents. Not so bad. I'll tell you what: I'm quite sure it'll be all right, since Mr. Cragg said he'd leave the whole thing up to me, but just to be on the safe side, I'd better run back to his office and show him the samples . . . "

"Sure," said the printer. "Just take a couple of these along."

"I'll do that," said Johnny, gathering up the samples, "but look, couldn't you just set up a couple of lines and run off a sample card like this, with Mr. Cragg's name on it?" He smiled ruefully, "Mr. Cragg's the sort who goes for that sort of thing — likes to see his name in print."

The printer frowned. "Well, I dunno. Without a depos . . . "

"It'd cinch the order," Johnny said,

slyly. "I know Mr. Cragg . . . "

"All right," sighed the printer. He went to a type case, set type rapidly for a moment or two, then carried the stick to the block. He made it ready in a small chase, took it to a tiny press and inside of three minutes came back with a neatly printed business card. He handed it to Johnny.

"Careful of the ink."

"Swell," said Johnny. "Shows the kind of work you can do. I'll run right over to the office now and get the okay. I may telephone you, but if not I'll be back this way inside of an hour or two."

"Thank you, sir," said the printer gratefully.

Outside, Sam said bitterly, "I didn't say a word — not a word."

"I know, Sam."

" . . . Even when you used my name."

Johnny chuckled. "I'm saving mine."

They were heading back toward the hotel — and the *California Credit*

Clothiers. "Feel like a suit yourself, Sam?"

"No!" cried Sam. "I don't like this old bag I'm wearing, but I like it a lot better'n I'd like stripes."

"Okay, then," grinned Johnny. "But I want you to look at a couple of neckties, or shirts or something. Just to hold the salesman a minute or so, when I get through with him . . . "

"What for?" Sam asked suspiciously. "I don't know what you're planning to pull . . . " Then he added hastily, "And I don't want to know."

"All right, it's just as well."

Johnny drew a deep breath and turned into the store of the *California Credit Clothiers*. It was a nice place, really a double-store, with a balcony for the overcoat department. But the suits were right on the first floor, and they had a good selection.

A man pounced on Johnny and Sam before the door had even swung shut. "Yes, gentlemen, a nice suit or topcoat, maybe?"

48

"A suit," said Johnny. "Something in a double-breasted — not too loud."

"We got some of the new worsted-tex here," said the salesman enthusiastically. "The latest patterns, right from New York. Look . . . " He did something to the rack that swung it out. "Here's a checked pattern . . . "

"I'm a salesman," said Johnny. "The kind of people I call on, I wouldn't want them to think I was a race track tout."

"No, sure, of course not. How about this blue pin-stripe? It's a honey."

"Not bad," said Johnny.

"Let's try it on for size."

Johnny was willing and the coat fitted quite well. It needed just a bit more room through the shoulders, which the salesman assured Johnny could be altered in a jiffy. So Johnny went into a dressing room to put on the trousers, while the salesman gave Sam the business. But when Johnny came out, wearing the trousers and coat, Sam was still shaking his head.

"Say!" exclaimed the salesman to Johnny. "That's a suit for you. Looks like a seventy-five dollar model. You wouldn't think it was only fifty-nine fifty, would you . . . Oh, Elmer!"

Elmer had a tape-measure about his neck and was obviously the fitter. He came over, pulled a little here and there, made a soap-chalk mark or two and nodded. "A very nice fit. You'll like it, Mister."

"How soon can I have it?"

"Tomorrow."

Johnny shook his head. "No. This afternoon."

"Couldn't possibly make it."

"Wait a minute," said Johnny. He went to the dressing room, got his pinned-up trousers. The tailor and the salesman both exclaimed.

"I'm just coming in from Denver, see," said Johnny. "There's a mixup over my luggage at the airport and then, wham, zowie, the steward catches a bag on my pants." He grinned. "See now why I got to have this suit today?"

"You could wear one of your other suits," the fitter suggested.

"That's it!" Johnny exclaimed. "The steward gave my luggage to a fellow named Simpson. He lives out in the Valley and weighs three hundred pounds. I've got his luggage and he's got mine — and we can't exchange until tomorrow . . . You've got to have this suit altered this afternoon, or else it's no deal . . . "

"Elmer," said the salesman. "You got to do it."

"All right," growled the fitter. "We got eighteen suits ahead, but in an emergency like this . . . "

"Thanks!" said Johnny. "I sure appreciate it."

He went back into the dressing room, put on his old suit and brought out the other. The salesman was filling out a sales blank.

"Your name, sir?"

"John Fletcher."

"You wish to take advantage of our generous credit terms . . . ?"

Johnny made a wry face. "A little poker game with a couple of buyers in Denver . . ."

The salesman chuckled. "It happens to all of us. Let's see . . . how about a twenty dollar deposit?"

"Mister," said Johnny, "I had just enough left to tip the taxicab driver. I've already put in my expense account, but the cashier won't give me the check for a day or two. How about paying the twenty the day after tomorrow . . ."

The salesman frowned mightily. "Couldn't you, ah, get an advance?"

Johnny winced. "And let the boss know I got took in a poker game? I'd rather patch these pants." He shook his head. "No, sir. Old Cragg would give me holy hell."

The salesman looked dubious. "Well, I don't know . . . You say you're a traveling salesman . . ."

"Not exactly. I do a lot of traveling for the firm — and I sell, naturally, when I can. But actually, I'm the assistant manager of the western division . . . " He grinned. "Look — why don't you call up Mr. Cragg? You can tell him I'm making a purchase. I'm sure he'll tell you I'm okay . . . But don't let on about the deposit. He might get suspicious about *that*. Just ask him about me in general . . . "

The salesman became happy once more. "All right, sir, if you don't mind . . . "

Johnny, reached into his pocket. "Here's my card . . . "

The salesman took it. "Thank you, sir."

"Then if everything's okay, I can stop in for the suit . . . about five o'clock?"

"Better make it five-thirty."

"Swell."

Johnny started for the door. Sam began to follow, then obeying his instructions, dawdled a moment at the sport coat section. The salesman stepped after him. Johnny, however, continued out of the store.

He walked leisurely until he was through the door, then sprinted across the street. He slackened speed in the hotel lobby, but headed immediately for the telephone booths.

There he got a shock. A woman was inside the one booth — the one that had the phone number of Hillcrest 1251. Johnny sweated for two long moments before the woman finally hung up and came out. Johnny promptly stepped into the booth and just as promptly, the phone rang.

"Transcontinental Terra Cotta Tile Corporation," Johnny said smoothly.

"Like to speak to Mr. Cragg," said a girl's voice.

"Who's calling?"

"The California Credit Clothiers . . . Mr. Bailey."

"Just a moment," said Johnny. He cleared his throat silently, then lowered his voice a couple of octaves. "Yes," he said into the mouthpiece, "Cragg talking."

"One moment please," said the girl's

voice. Then a man's voice came on. "Mr. Cragg? This is the California Credit Clothiers. We'd like to ask you about one of your employees, who's making a purchase here . . . "

"Yes, who is it?"

"A Mr. John Fletcher. Is he in your employ?"

"Oh yes," said Johnny. "One of our executives. Hmmph. Credit clothiers, you say? Funny, he'd be buying on credit . . . Is the amount very much?"

"In the neighborhood of sixty dollars. Ah, how long has Mr. Fletcher been in your employ."

"Oh, quite a long while," said Johnny. "Could be ten-eleven years. Don't remember exactly. Matter of fact, he was here, before I came out from Chicago to take charge of the Coast Office. Our best salesman; I made him assistant sales manager two years ago."

"Indeed? And, ah, would you care to tell me Mr. Fletcher's salary?"

"It's ample to pay cash for a suit of

clothes, if that's what you mean." Then, testily: "All right, I know Fletcher. Can't resist a poker game. Hmmph. He gets a hundred and thirty-five dollars a week. You'd think on that he'd be able to save some money, wouldn't you?"

"Yes, of course," said Mr. Bailey, of the *California Credit Clothiers*. "But we all have our little weaknesses, you know. In other words, then, you'd say that Mr. Fletcher was a good credit risk."

"The best," said Johnny curtly. "As good as myself."

"Thank you, sir, we're glad to hear that. Goodbye."

Johnny hung up the receiver and wiped the perspiration from his forehead. He looked through the glass door and saw Sam Cragg waiting outside. He opened the little door.

"You see," he said, "it's the build-up, that's all."

5

JOHNNY and Sam retired early that evening — the new suit from the *California Credit Clothiers* hanging safely in the closet. Sam pulled down the bed in the sitting room and Johnny luxuriated in the big double bed in the bedroom. It was ten-thirty.

At ten-thirty-five the argument started in the room across the court. It waxed vigorous and loud. Johnny endured it for ten minutes then went to the window.

"Cut out that racket!" he yelled.

If anything the argument became louder. The window across the way was raised but the shade was pulled down almost to the sill so that Johnny could not see into the room. From the voices, however, it seemed to him that two or three men and at least one woman were involved in the argument.

He leaned out of the window.

"Cut out that noise!" he roared. "Cut it out or I'll come over and give you something to yammer about."

The window shade across the way flew up and a stringy, weather-beaten man of about fifty stuck out his head. "You and who else?" he cried.

"Me and me alone," Johnny retorted.

"Oh yeah?" The stringy man drew back. His arm came forward and something flew from his hand.

In panic, Johnny jerked back. A foot above his head, glass crashed. The falling shards missed him only because of his agility.

"Why, you . . . !" he gasped. He whirled and headed for the door in the sitting room. Before he reached it he collided with Sam Cragg.

"What's the trouble?" Sam cried.

"Guy across the way heaved a rock through my window. I'm going over to murder him." Johnny side-stepped Sam and tore open the door.

He traveled six feet. Big Tim

O'Hanlon, the house detective, was just stepping out of the elevator.

"Hey, Fletcher!" he called.

Johnny retreated to the doorway of his suite. Before he could close the door, O'Hanlon charged forward.

"What's the idee chasing around the hall in your underwear?" the detective cried.

"Who, me?" Johnny asked innocently.

"Yas, you — and look, while we're on the subject, there wasn't any horse named Mr. Copperman running today. What do you think of that?"

"Isn't today Tuesday?" Johnny asked.

"You know damn well it's Thursday."

"Thursday! How time flies. Well, Mr. Copperman will be running again next Tuesday."

"So will you." O'Hanlon bared his teeth. "You know what I think about you? I think you're a slicker. I got a tip that you checked in with a suitcase full of bricks . . ."

Johnny drew himself together. "Do you want to force your way into my room and find out?" he asked coldly.

O'Hanlon hesitated. Johnny clinched it. "In the morning, sir, I'll ask the manager if it is customary for the employees of this hotel to insult the guests. In the meantime — good night!" He slammed the door in the house detective's face.

He went into the bedroom. "Okay, Sam!"

Sam came out of the closet. "That was a close call," he said, exhaling heavily.

"Tomorrow," Johnny promised grimly, "tomorrow I'm going to pin back that bellboy's ears." He looked at the floor, then stooped suddenly and picked up the stone the man across the way had heaved through the window.

He whistled. "Heft, this, Sam!"

Sam took the stone. "Cripes, it's heavy! Feels like it's iron . . . or something."

Johnny took back the stone and scratched it with a thumbnail. "Or something." He shook his head. "I'm a monkey's uncle if this isn't a chunk of silver ore . . . "

"Silver!"

"It must be almost pure, too. It weighs at least twenty pounds and is only about three or four inches thick."

"How much is it worth?"

"That's hard to say. Silver's around fifty cents an ounce. Let's say it's only fifty per cent silver — about ten pounds — that would make it eighty dollars."

"Only eighty dollars? You'd think a nugget like that'd be worth thousands."

"If it was gold."

"Maybe it is."

"No, it's black. Silver's black in its native state . . . or is it?"

Johnny went to the window. The room across the court was dark. He turned back to Sam.

"We'll find out in the morning."

Johnny Fletcher did not sleep well, despite the big, comfortable bed. His conscience was heavy. Yet he was only half dressed in the morning when there was a loud knock on the door. Muttering, he went into the sitting room and shook Sam.

"We're about to be evicted," he said. "Get up."

Sam groaned and jumped out of bed. "What a life!"

Johnny went to the door and jerked it open.

The man standing there was the stringy one from across the way. He was grinning foolishly. "Hello, neighbor. Mind if I step in?"

"If you don't mind getting a knuckle massage," Johnny said, belligerently.

"Well now, I don't think that'll be necessary," said the man in the doorway. "On account of I only came over to apologize for losing my temper last night." He beamed and held out a gnarled hand. "My name's Dan Tompkins."

Johnny took the hand. "I'm Johnny Fletcher." He led the way into the sitting room. "And this is Sam Cragg."

Sam was wearing shorts, nothing else.

Tompkins regarded him admiringly. "You got's good a build as that doggone Cotter."

"Cotter?" Johnny asked quickly.

"The guy was doing all the arguing with me last night — Joe Cotter."

"Jeez!" said Sam.

"Joe Cotter's here at the hotel?" Johnny demanded.

"Uh-huh. You know Joe?"

"I'll murder him," Sam said thickly.

Tompkins showed interest. "Well, now, we might make a deal. How much you figure the job's worth?"

"Are you kidding?" Johnny asked.

"Not me, gents. Where I come from we don't joke about murder. I don't like Cotter and I'm willing to pay a fair amount to have him rubbed out. If I was ten-fifteen years younger I'd do the job myself. But Joe's pretty tough. What do you say to five hundred?" He looked at Johnny. "All right, seven-fifty. But that's my top offer. The job ain't worth more than that."

"We'll talk it over, Tompkins,"

Johnny said. "Now, if you'll excuse us . . ."

"Oh, sure. That wasn't what I really came over for, though. It was about that — that piece — I threw through your window last night."

"Oh, forget that. I'll tell the management to put the window on your bill. Okay?"

"I guess so — but that ain't all. That chunk of rock I threw — I'd like to have it back."

"Why, I'm afraid I threw it out."

"You didn't!"

"It was only a stone . . ."

Tompkins exclaimed. "It was solid silver, that's what it was. Worth three hundred dollars if it was worth a nickel . . . Where did you throw it?"

"I don't remember." Johnny pursed up his lips. "Three hundred dollars . . . are you sure?"

"Naturally. And I've got to find it."

"If it was so valuable why'd you throw it?"

"'Cause I lost my temper. I'm that

way. Out in Arizona they cross the street when I'm drunk, 'cause I'm too doggone mean."

"A man ought to learn to control his temper," Johnny said, sanctimoniously. "It pays in the long run. Take this case — you throw away something worth three hundred dollars. Now, it'll probably cost you about a hundred and fifty to get it back."

"Huh?"

"Naturally, you'd pay that much — as a reward — wouldn't you?"

"Say . . . !" cried Tompkins. "I'm beginnin' to think . . . "

"Don't!" said Johnny.

Tompkins glowered at Johnny for a moment. Then he shrugged. "All right, I know when I'm licked. A hundred bucks!"

"A hundred and fifty."

"It ain't really worth three hundred. I was just talking . . . "

"Talking costs money."

Tompkins groaned. "I never will learn to keep my mouth shut." He dug into his trousers pocket and brought out a roll of bills. He peeled off three — all fifties. Johnny took them and went into the bedroom. After a moment he returned with the lump of silver.

Tompkins grinned and produced a revolver. "There's more'n one way to skin a cat . . . "

Sam Cragg — almost lazily — reached out and slapped Tompkins' hand. The gun hit the floor with a thud. Tompkins howled and leaped back, clutching his right hand with his left.

"Mustn't," Sam chided.

"Jumpin' tarantulas!" cried Dan Tompkins. "What've I run up against?"

"Just a couple of boys trying to make an honest living," Johnny said. "Sit down and we'll talk things over.

"What else is there to talk about?"

"You're in trouble," Johnny continued. "You said this Joe Cotter's in your hair. Well, we don't like him either. Maybe we can pool our interests."

"I dunno what your trouble with him

is," said Tompkins. "Can't be the same as mine, though."

"You never can tell. You didn't happen to stop over in San Bernardino the night before last, did you?"

"Me? No. But I know somebody who did."

"Let's talk about it."

Sam was trying to catch Johnny's eye, but the latter refused to look. He went to the pull-down bed and seated himself on it. After a moment, Tompkins crossed to an armchair. Sam groaned and headed for the bathroom.

"About Joe Cotter," Johnny said. "He's from your part of Arizona?"

"Yeah. He's from Tombstone. I make Hansonville my headquarters."

"Hansonville," Johnny mused. "I thought that place was a ghost town."

"It is — pretty near. But she was plenty lively in the old days."

"So I've read. The town's just a few miles from Tombstone?"

"'Bout twelve. Well, sir, you were going to tell me about Joe Cotter."

67

"No, *you* were going to tell *me* about him. He's your enemy."

"He's yours, too."

"All right," Johnny conceded. "But we're not going to get anywhere if you don't lay all your cards on the table."

"Sure," grinned Tompkins. "You were saying something about San Bernardino. Uh, there was somethin' in the paper about somethin' that happened there yesterday morning. Seems the police found a car over by Fontana which had a dead man in it." Tompkins paused. "Fella name of Kitchen. Lemme see, Hugh Kitchen."

"Never heard of him. But I was coming through San Bernardino the other night and saw this Joe Cotter pulling into a motel."

Dan Tompkins showed interest. "The name of that place couldn't have been *El Toreador*, could it?"

"It could."

Tompkins was silent a moment. Then he gave Johnny a shrewd glance.

"Mister," he said, "I don't know you from Geronimo. What's your business?"

"Why," said Johnny, "I'm a sort of detective."

Sam Cragg, coming out of the bathroom, exclaimed, "Nix, Johnny!"

"Pay no attention to Sam," Johnny said to Tompkins. "He never wants me to take cases unless there's a big retainer. You wouldn't think to look at him that he's one of the best operators in the business."

"Well, he looks plenty strong. And he'll need strength if he's going to go up against Joe Cotter. They say Joe's the strongest man in Arizona . . . "

"That's because Sam isn't there." Johnny picked up the Los Angeles phone directory. "Sam!" He tossed the book to Sam.

Sam caught it and with a quick jerk ripped it in half. Then he took each section and tore it across again. Dan Tompkins whistled softly.

"See what I mean," Johnny said.

69

"Now if you'll give me a little retainer . . . "

"You already got one-fifty!"

"That was for something else. However, I'll take it into consideration. Another fifty and we're working for you."

Tompkins looked at Johnny for a moment, then began chuckling. "Fletcher, I like you."

"I like you, too. The fifty . . . ?"

Tompkins reached for his roll and peeled off an additional fifty. Johnny stowed it away with its mates. "Now, let's have it — the whole story."

"It's a silver mine," said Tompkins.

"You found one?"

"Not exactly. It's been there all the time. Only it ain't been worked since around 1886. You might rightly call it deserted. That's why I figure she ought to be mine."

"But it actually belongs to someone else?"

Tompkins scowled. "A girl who happens to be the grandniece of Old

Jim Walker. He willed it to her. But what he actually willed was a worthless hole in the ground. Walker didn't know that I spent two years poking around in the old shafts, working my fingers to the bone, risking my life . . . "

"All right," Johnny conceded. "You worked like a dog and you struck pay dirt . . . what then?"

"I wanted to do the right thing. Jim Walker hadn't taken an ounce of silver out of the mine since 1886. But he did own it . . . so I wrote him, offering to buy the mine from him — for a reasonable price. I didn't know he had shoved off. So then I get this letter from his grandson, Charles Ralston . . . "

"I thought you said a grandniece owned the mine?"

"That's right — Helen Walker. But I didn't find that out until later. You got to know the setup. Ten years ago Old Jim Walker was worth about ten million dollars. He retired, turning his affairs over to his son-in-law. The depression came along and said son-in-law lost every dollar of the old boy's money. Not only that but he made things miserable for Old Jim, so that finally Jim went to live with his nephew's widow . . . When he died six months ago he willed the only thing he still owned — this mine — to the widow's daughter, Helen Walker.

"But when I wrote to Jim — not knowing he was dead — his grandson got the letter. Young Ralston smelled a chance to make some money and tried to buy the mine from his cousin, Helen Walker. The girl wouldn't sell, then right away Ralston got suspicious. He got a lawyer by the name of Kitchen . . . "

"Ah yes," said Johnny. "The man in San Bernardino."

"That's right. Only Ralston claims he don't know a thing about it."

"You mean Ralston's here in Hollywood?"

"It was him I was arguin' with last night. Him and Cotter."

"Where does Joe Cotter come in?"

Dan Tompkins grimaced. "That was where I made my first mistake. I didn't know how to locate Old Jim Walker and I asked Joe to trace him for me . . . He's a sort of a lawyer . . . Now Joe's trying to squeeze in . . . Well, that's the story up to date."

Johnny frowned. "I don't see where there should be any complications. Helen Walker owns the mine and if she wants to sell — "

"That's just it!" Tompkins cried. "Old Jim willed the mine to Helen, but Ralston claims now that the old man was crazy or something and says that since he's Walker's nearest relative the mine shoulda come to him. That's where the lawyers come in."

"I see." Johnny nodded thoughtfully. "And *you* weren't in San Bernardino the night before last?"

"Nope!"

"You can prove it?"

"Ain't my word good enough?" Tompkins exclaimed angrily.

"To me, yes, but it may not be good enough for the police."

"What've the police got to do with this?"

Johnny shook his head. "Police are funny. They ask questions. I wouldn't be a bit surprised if they started asking *me* questions."

Across the room, Sam Cragg winced.

"I don't like police," Tompkins growled. "I never got nothing good from them. I'm paying you to keep them off my neck."

"I'll do my best, old man. Now just what is it you want me to do in this affair?"

"Ain't I been telling you for the last fifteen minutes? I want to buy this silver mine."

"For a thousand dollars?"

"I'll go higher — maybe even up to three thousand."

"That's very generous of you," Johnny said drily. "How much is the mine worth?"

"To anybody else — nothing."

"But if there's silver in it as rich as that lump . . . "

"Ain't you ever been in a silver mine?" Tompkins exclaimed. "The Silver Tombstone's six hundred feet deep — there're six levels and each one has about fifty shafts running all around underground — like a honeycomb. If you don't know where to look for this vein I uncovered you'll have a sweet time finding enough silver to fill a tooth . . . 'Course since they know it's there they can dig around and eventually they'll find it, but it's going to cost them a lot of money."

"But if Helen Walker won't sell you the mine you can't work it."

"That's about the size of it. But she won't get anything out of it, either. She's broke. She can't spend any money to blast around. Cost her fifty-sixty thousand."

"Why don't you offer to split with her?"

"I did. I made her a fifty-fifty proposition, but she wouldn't listen.

Says Jim Walker wanted her to have the mine all for herself and that's the way she's going to have it. That's what you've got to talk her out of — and keep the other guys away from her."

"She's staying here at the hotel?"

"No — she's at the Manhattan. Cotter's staying here — and Ralston."

Johnny nodded thoughtfully. "If talk can make her change her mind . . . "

"And if talkin' ain't any good, you'll . . . ?" Tompkins leaned forward eagerly.

"I'll what?"

The prospector slapped Johnny's knee. "I leave it to you, eh?"

"Yeah . . . just relax."

Tompkins inhaled heavily. "I guess I can — now. You two fit the fortune teller's description — "

"Fortune teller?" Sam exclaimed. "You believe in fortune tellers?"

"Why not? Some people've got the gift — "

"Bunk!" scoffed Sam. "Nobody can

look in a glass ball and tell you anything. It's the stars . . . "

Tompkins blinked. "What stars?"

"Why, the stars in the skies . . . When were you born?"

"May 26th, 1888 . . . "

Sam whipped out his astrology book. Johnny chuckled as he watched his friend turn the pages.

"May 26th," Sam repeated. "That's Gemini . . . yeah, sure . . . this is your lucky period. You're all right — if you watch yourself and don't have business dealings with strangers."

Tompkins grunted. "It says that in your book? Madame Zarini told me just the opposite. Said good fortune was going to come to me through two strangers . . . Of course, if you're going to believe *your* book . . . "

Johnny struck Sam's shoulder. "Put that book away or I'll make you see some stars. There's work to be done — "

Sam put away his book. "What work?"

"You're coming with me to see Helen Walker."

Tompkins was regarding Sam with a peevish look, but Johnny herded him and Sam out of the room. They left Tompkins in the corridor and descended to the hotel lobby.

As they stepped out of the elevator a suave, neatly dressed man with a white carnation in his lapel called to Johnny. "Mr. Fletcher . . . !"

Just behind the suave man, Big Tim O'Hanlon leaned against a pillar, grinning wickedly.

"Mr. Fletcher," said the man with the carnation. "I'm Mr. Stuart, the manager. I'm sorry to inform you that a mistake was made yesterday in giving you the suite. It is our custom to ask for, ah, payment in advance on suites . . . "

"I see," said Johnny grimly. "Well, if that is the custom of the hotel — how much is my suite per week?"

"Per week?" Mr. Stuart seemed surprised. "Why, ah, there's a ten per cent discount ... Sixty-three dollars."

Johnny pulled out two fifties. "Please credit me with the balance."

Mr. Stuart's mouth fell open. Then he became all fluttery. "I, ah, Mr. Fletcher, I, ah, I'm sorry I had to mention this to you. A little mistake, ah, perhaps ... "

"Perhaps," said Johnny. "And now, since we're talking about customs and rules and regulations, do you mind if I make a suggestion? It's customary in the better hotels — as you may have heard — to invite criticisms of service, et cetera ... "

"Oh, by all means. I would greatly appreciate any suggestions."

"Well, it's just this — shortly after I checked into my suite yesterday a large, uncouth individual knocked on my door and under the pretext of being the house detective — an imposter, of course — hinted that he knew a good thing in a horse race and — "

"No!" cried Mr. Stuart.

Johnny raised his shoulders expressively. "I could hardly believe it myself. Such brazen touting! I knew he couldn't be the house detective, yet — " He blinked. "Why I do believe that's the man over there . . . "

Mr. Stuart whirled and saw O'Hanlon. He started toward him. Johnny gestured to Sam. "Come along, old boy. Mustn't be contaminated . . . "

"Serves him right," growled Sam.

6

THE Manhattan was less than a mile from the Fremont, but Johnny Fletcher was in an expansive mood. He took a taxi and when he reached the Manhattan got involved in a complicated business of obtaining change for a fifty dollar bill. By the time the taxi bill was settled a good number of the employees of the hotel — as well as some guests in the lobby — were aware that an important man had arrived. A man who had nothing smaller than fifty dollar bills.

The clerk violated a hotel rule by giving Johnny the number of Miss Helen Walker's room.

Johnny knocked on the door of her room on the fifth floor. It was opened by the girl from New York . . . whose flat tire Sam Cragg had changed on the road from San Bernardino.

She recognized Johnny and her blue eyes flashed sparks.

"Hello," Johnny said lamely.

She started to close the door in his face, but couldn't for Johnny's bookselling technique was ever with him and he got his foot in the door. Helen Walker promptly kicked his shin. Johnny exclaimed in pain but put his shoulder to the door and pushed.

It was opened suddenly and Johnny practically fell into the arms of a tall, lean young man of about thirty.

The man grabbed Johnny by the shoulder. "Here, you, what're you trying to do?"

Sam Cragg crowded in behind Johnny, squeezed past him and knocked the tall man's hand from Johnny. "Easy does it, chum!"

The man blocking the door called back into the room. "Call the desk!"

"Now, wait a minute," Johnny said quickly. "Let's talk this thing over."

"There's nothing to talk about!" exclaimed the tall man. "You're trying to break into this room and — "

"Let them in, Mike," said Helen Walker.

Mike hesitated then retreated into the room. Johnny and Sam followed — and discovered that there was still another person in the room; a girl about the same age as Helen Walker and just about as pretty although in a more outdoorsy way. She was dark; hair almost black and skin tanned by a thousand suns.

"All right," said Helen Walker. "Let's have it — or I *will* call the manager."

"First," said Johnny, "I want to apologize for the joke I perpetrated on you yesterday." He reached into his pocket and brought out some money. Extracting a dollar and a quarter he extended it to Helen Walker.

Her lips parted. "What's that for?"

"The joke. You didn't think I was serious in asking you to pay for changing that tire?"

She said sharply. "Now listen . . . "

"Ha-ha-ha," Johnny laughed. "When

I saw your New York license I was so tickled to see someone from home I couldn't resist pulling that corny joke. Then, when I saw that you hadn't gotten it, I tried to explain but you went off too quickly . . . "

"Say!" exclaimed the man known as Mike. "Are these those two hoboes you were telling us about?"

"Hoboes!" cried Sam.

"They're the ones," said Helen Walker.

Johnny shook his head sadly. "See — that's what a joke'll do. A hobo!" He sighed wearily. "Let's start at the beginning. My name is Johnny Fletcher and this is Sam Cragg."

Mike glared at Johnny. But the suntanned girl suddenly held out her hand. "I'm Laura Henderson and I'm glad to know you, Johnny Fletcher."

"Likewise," said Johnny, taking the girl's hand.

"And Mike is my brother," Laura went on.

Mike Henderson ignored Johnny's

proffered hand. "All right," he said, "just for the sake of argument, let's call it a joke. Now, is there anything else you've got to say? Or do I have to throw you both out?"

"Try it," growled Sam.

"Well," said Johnny. "I was hoping to talk privately to Miss Walker . . . about the Silver Tombstone . . . "

"What do you know about the Silver Tombstone?" gasped Helen Walker.

"I'd like to buy it."

Helen Walker looked at Mike Henderson. Henderson nodded. "What do you know about the Silver Tombstone?" he demanded.

"I want to buy it."

"This is too much for me," Helen Walker said and seated herself suddenly.

"Where'd you hear about the Silver Tombstone?" Henderson asked harshly.

"Do I have to tell that?" Johnny looked innocently at Henderson. "When you go into a grocery store to buy some oranges the man doesn't ask you where you heard about oranges . . . "

"This is no time for clowning, Fletcher," Henderson said, through clenched teeth. "Only about four people know about the Silver Tombstone and I want to know . . ."

"Who're the four?"

Henderson made a savage gesture. "We're not going to get anywhere that way."

"No," Johnny admitted. He looked down at Helen Walker. "I am prepared to pay you three thousand dollars for the Silver Tombstone . . ."

"A hobo," Laura said suddenly. "A hobo with three thousand dollars. This is getting interesting."

"I'm not interested in selling anything, Helen Walker said evenly.

"That's final?"

"Definitely."

Johnny sighed. "Too bad. I've always wanted to own a silver mine . . . By the way, you didn't happen to stop the night before last at a motel in San Bernardino — a place called *El Toreador?*"

Helen Walker sat very still for a moment, then she stood up. "What are you driving at?"

"Nothing, particularly. Only we stopped there ourselves that night and along about one A.M someone screamed in the cabin next to ours — a woman . . . "

"Get out of here!"

"That's all," said Mike Henderson firmly.

"Okay, Buster," Johnny said, laconically. He signaled to Sam Cragg.

"Buster," repeated Laura Henderson. "I must remember that."

Johnny grinned. "I'll give you a ring sometime, Miss Henderson."

Sam passed out into the hall. Johnny followed more leisurely, but the slamming door almost hit him.

7

AS they walked toward the elevators Sam gave Johnny a withering look. "Got enough?"

"Why should I have?" Johnny retorted. "This is still easier than working — and better paying."

"Yes, but you live longer if you work."

The elevator door opened and they stepped in. They rode down in silence. As they stepped out to the lobby, Sam exclaimed.

"Joe Cotter!"

Johnny had already seen him. The Arizonian was coming across the lobby toward them. "What're you fellows doing here?" he demanded.

Johnny looked around. "Why, this is a hotel, isn't it?"

"It is — an expensive one. Don't tell me *you're* staying here!"

"No, we're not, but we dropped in to see a friend — on the fifth floor. Miss Walker."

Cotter's eyes narrowed. "Are you kidding?"

"Not at all. Matter of fact I'm trying to buy a mine from her, a silver mine."

The man from Arizona bared his teeth. "There's something awfully fishy about you two . . . I think I'll check up on you."

"Could I recommend a good private detective?" Johnny asked.

Joe Cotter reached out and took a handful of Johnny's coat. Sam Cragg growled and grabbed Cotter's right wrist. The big man let go of Johnny. His eyes went to Sam.

"All right, you're asking for it and you're going to get it."

Sam sneered. "When?"

"Maybe sooner than you expect. And don't think I've forgotten about that twenty-five you owe me." Cotter glowered once more at Sam and

Johnny, then stepped into a waiting elevator.

"I don't like that, guy," Sam said to Johnny. "I don't like him a lot."

"I'm not exactly in love with him myself."

They left the hotel, Johnny so absorbed in thought he did not see the line of waiting taxicabs. As a result they walked back to the Fremont.

As they entered the hotel and bore down upon the elevators, Tim O'Hanlon got up from a chair behind a potted palm. There was an ugly look on the house detective's face. Johnny, seeing it, veered away and went to the desk.

"What room has Charles Ralston got?" he asked the clerk.

The man nodded toward the house phone. "Call his room, please." Then he recognized Johnny. "Oh, Mr. Fletcher," he said, respectfully. "Mr. Ralston's occupying Room 1116. Shall I ring him for you?"

"Don't bother." Johnny nodded thanks

and headed for the elevators. Passing O'Hanlon he grinned and jerked his head toward the desk. O'Hanlon looked and saw the clerk watching. He muttered under his breath and returned to his seat.

Sam was waiting for Johnny at the elevators. "Eleven," Johnny said as he stepped in. Sam looked at him inquiringly.

On the eleventh floor Johnny discovered that 1116 was directly opposite the elevators. He knocked on the door. There was no response.

Sam nodded toward the elevator. "Nobody home."

Johnny shrugged and knocked again. Inside the room a voice cried out in agony. "Go 'way'n lemme alone!"

Johnny chuckled and beat a tattoo upon the door. After a moment it was opened by a man in purple pajamas and the worst hangover Johnny had ever seen.

"What the devil do you want?" Charles Ralston cried.

"Talk, Charlie," Johnny said and brushed past Ralston into the room.

"I like to talk," Ralston groaned. "But not this early in the morning. Besides — I don't know you men."

"Simple. I'll introduce us. This is Sam Cragg and I'm Johnny Fletcher. And you're Charlie Ralston."

Ralston gripped his head in both hands and sat down on the edge of his rumpled bed. "Excuse me if I fail to show any enthusiasm."

"Oh, that's all right," Johnny said, making himself comfortable in a chair. "I'll do most of the talking anyway."

"You always do," Sam Cragg said.

Johnny gave him a sharp glance. Then he gave his full attention to Charles Ralston. "Charlie, just how much would you pay for the Silver Tombstone?"

"Pay? I own it now . . . " Then he lowered his hands from his head. "Say — who're you?"

"I just told you — Johnny Fletcher."

"I heard the name, but who, rather *what* are you?"

"You mean you never heard of me?" Johnny shrugged. "Well, such is fame. But then come to think of it, you've lived in New York all your life. The point is, Helen Walker is the legal owner of the mine . . . "

"That remains to be seen," Ralston retorted. "I admit that my grandfather mentioned her in his will, but that will was made under duress . . . "

"Okay," said Johnny, "let the lawyers fight that out. And let them split the Silver Tombstone among themselves — for their fees."

Ralston scowled. "What's the idea . . . ?"

"The idea is that one of your lawyers, Hugh Kitchen, has already been murdered . . . "

"What do you know about Hugh Kitchen?" cried Ralston.

"I know that he was murdered in a motel in San Bernardino. And I know that he would be alive today if he hadn't been messed up in this mine -and-will fight of yours."

"Are you a policeman?" Ralston cried.

Johnny made a deprecating gesture, dismissing the accusation. "Mr. Ralston, murder breeds murder. And we don't want any more murders . . . So . . . how much will *you* take to withdraw your claim — whatever the right or wrong of it — to your grandfather's estate?"

Ralston looked at Johnny a moment. Then he shook his head. "Who sent you here?"

"That's beside the point."

"All right, you won't tell. Then I'll give you my answer. I'll take half a million dollars."

Johnny nodded. "Let me reverse the process, now. How much will *you* pay for Helen Walker's claim?"

"Nothing."

Johnny sighed wearily. "We're not going to get very far this way . . . "

"No, we're not."

Johnny got up from his chair and in doing so knocked a book off the edge of a dresser. It fell to the floor. Johnny picked it up, saw that the title was *Tombstone Days*. The author's name was Jason Lord. He put the book back on the dresser.

"Very well, Mr. Ralston, I will bid you good Good morning."

"Good-bye," said Ralston firmly.

Johnny went out, followed by Sam. As they were waiting for the elevator Sam sniffed. "What a nice waste of time that was."

"Oh, I wouldn't say that, Sam."

The elevator door opened and they got in.

"Five," said Sam.

"No, lobby," Johnny corrected.

They got out in the lobby, dodged Tim O'Hanlon once more and went to the street. For a half block or so Sam walked in silence beside Johnny. Then he could stand it no longer.

"What're you up to, Johnny?" he cried.

Johnny yawned. "Oh, I'm a little tired. I thought I'd pick up a book and catch up on my reading. Ah — here's a store."

He led the way into a small bookstore.

A mild-mannered clerk descended upon them.

"I'd like to get a book called *Tombstone Days*," Johnny said.

The clerk shook his head. "I'm afraid we don't have it. Who's it by?"

"Jason Lord."

"Mmm, I don't believe I've ever heard of it. But I'll look it up."

He went to a huge index, turned pages and finally shook his head. "It isn't even listed. How old a book is it?"

"I don't know exactly. Fairly old, I would say."

"Then the book is undoubtedly out of print. You may have to get it from a rare book dealer . . . Why don't you try Eisenschiml's place? It's right across the street."

"Thanks, I'll do that."

They left the store, crossed the street and found a store with lettering on the window: *Oscar Eisenschiml, Out of Print Books, Autographs, Prints*.

They went into the musty-smelling

store. In the rear of a shop a bald, heavy-set man in his early sixties was seated in an old-fashioned rocking chair, reading a yellowed pamphlet. He did not even look up.

Johnny winked at Sam and started toward the back of the shop. "I say," he said, "I'd like to get a book called *Tombstone Days*, by Jason Lord."

"So would I," said Oscar Eisenschiml, still keeping his eyes on his pamphlet.

Johnny drew a deep breath. "I'll pay up to ten dollars for the book — if you can get it for me quick."

Eisenschiml finally lowered his pamphlet and sized up Johnny. "Are you kidding?" he asked, bluntly.

"No, I'll pay the price."

"Ten dollars?"

"Yes."

Eisenschiml got up, went to a rolltop desk and picked up a paper-covered book. He riffled the pages, came to one and read a moment. "Yes," he said, "a copy of *Tombstone Days* was sold in 1927 for six hundred and fifty dollars." He looked at Johnny. "And you're willing to pay ten dollars for another copy."

Johnny looked discomfited. "We live and learn. I heard about the book and since I'm interested in Tombstone, I thought I'd like to read about it."

"You can buy a good book on Tombstone for seventy-nine cents," the book dealer said. "Probably a lot better than the Lord book."

"Have you got one — the seventy-nine cent one?"

Eisenschiml looked at him in disgust. "There's a dump across the street where you can probably pick one up."

"The dump across the street sent me over here," Johnny said, drily.

"Yes? Well, tell 'em to keep their customers," grunted Eisenschiml. He returned to his rocking chair and picked up his yellowed pamphlet. "Wastin' my time!"

Johnny and Sam left the store. Outside Sam whistled. "Imagine a guy like Ralston payin' six hundred and fifty bucks just for a book!"

"It isn't right," said Johnny. "It isn't right or fair . . . Come in here."

Sam looked at the window of the store Johnny was already entering and uttered a startled exclamation. Then he went into the store after Johnny.

Johnny was already showing a key to the proprietor. "Like to have a key made like this one — only a little different."

"Like this, only different?" The locksmith turned Johnny's key over and over in his hands. "Looks like a hotel key . . . "

"Does it? It's for the door of my wine cellar. The last butler I had walked off with it. I changed the lock, just in case he should come back some night and then I lost the new key. But it's something like this one — I bought two locks at the time; this one's for my wife's fur vault . . . "

"I can't make a key without having a duplicate key — or the number of the lock."

"I wanted to get the number, but it was too dark down in the basement." Johnny smiled pleasantly. The locksmith gave him a sour look and taking Johnny's key, walked down a ways behind his counter. He studied several huge bunches of keys, finally took one down and began pawing over the individual keys. At last he took a key from the ring. He brought it to Johnny and dropped it on the counter, along with Johnny's own key.

"Fifty cents," he grunted.

Johnny picked up the two keys. "You're sure it'll fit?"

"Of course it'll fit. It's a master key of that series. I shouldn't ought to sell it, on account of that other key sure 'nough looks like a hotel key and if the hotel association finds out . . ."

"Thanks," said Johnny hastily and dropped a half dollar on the counter.

Sam could scarcely wait until they reached the sidewalk before he whirled on Johnny.

"What're you going to do, Johnny?

That was your hotel key."

"That's right," said Johnny. "I want to read *Tombstone Days* and since I haven't got six-fifty to buy a copy, I thought — "

"No!" howled Sam. "You can't do that . . . "

"Maybe I can't," said Johnny. "But I'm sure going to try." He took a nickel from his pocket and extended it to Sam. "He doesn't know your voice so run into that drugstore there and telephone him . . . "

"I won't!"

"Telephone Charlie Ralston. Tell him . . . " Johnny thought rapidly. "Tell him you're the county morgue and that he *must* come down immediately and identify the body of Hugh Kitchen. No, not identify. He may have done that already. They want to ask him some questions. And while you're about it, look up the address of the morgue."

Sam gave Johnny a bitter look, then he took the nickel and went into the drugstore. He was gone about two minutes. When he came out he nodded gloomily.

"I think he took the bait, but I'm not sure . . . "

"What's the address of the morgue?"

"Two-eleven West Temple."

Johnny nodded. "A good half hour each way by taxicab. Five minutes in the morgue. A safe hour. Not enough, but I'll read fast." He took a five dollar bill from his pocket. "To be on the safe side, you'd better follow him. See that he goes to the morgue. If he doesn't and there's danger of him coming back sooner than I expect you'll have to telephone me in the room."

"All right," Sam said hopelessly. "I'll go all the way . . . but I don't like it."

"I don't either," retorted Johnny.

As they neared the hotel — on the opposite side of the street — the doorman blew his whistle for a cab. As it pulled up, Charles Ralston crossed the sidewalk.

"Go to it, Sam," said Johnny,

clapping his friend on the back.

Sam started across the street. Johnny waited until he had climbed into a second taxi, then he crossed and entered the hotel.

This time Tim O'Hanlon was not in the lobby. Johnny got into the elevator, rode up to the fifth floor, then climbed six flights of stairs to the eleventh. The corridor was deserted when he reached it and Johnny stepped quickly to the door of Room 1116.

The newly-purchased key fitted perfectly and a moment later he was in the room. He bolted the door on the inside, went into the room proper and picked up the copy of *Tombstone Days*. Seating himself in a chair he turned to the title page. It read: *Tombstone days, Being an account of the fabulous boom town of Tombstone in Arizona Territory. By Jason Lord, a resident of Tombstone from its earliest days. Copyright 1889.*

Johnny settled back in his chair and began reading. The first chapter told of the discovery of gold on the site of Tombstone, by Ed Schiefelin, a former Army scout. The second chapter continued with Schiefelin's adventures in the early days of the mining camp. Then the story swung into the boom town days of Tombstone, the coming of the honky-tonk, the gambler and bad man and the resultant peace officers, who were sometimes . . .

At that point the telephone rang and Johnny Fletcher jumped about six inches. Two chapters, three . . . he couldn't have been in the room more than ten or fifteen minutes. Charles Ralston wouldn't even be at the morgue by this time.

Johnny picked up the phone. He said, cautiously: "Yes?"

"Ralston?" asked a voice.

8

JOHNNY blinked at the telephone receiver. The voice definitely was not that of Sam Cragg. In fact, it sounded muffled, hoarse; a disguised voice.

"Yeah," Johnny said, making his own voice hoarse.

It was the wrong thing to do. The voice on the wire tumbled. "Who is this?" it demanded. "It isn't Ralston."

"It's the house detective," Johnny retorted.

"The house detec . . . " began the voice on the wire, then stopped. A click sounded in Johnny's ear and the wire went dead.

Johnny hung up, scowled at the phone a moment, then looked at the door. His position was precarious. In a matter of moments he could be discovered.

But he hadn't yet found what he hoped to find in the ancient book. Well, there was only one thing to do. Johnny did it. He picked up the book, slipped it under his coat and departed.

There was no one in the hall and it wasn't until he was descending from the seventh to the sixth floor that he encountered anyone — Bellboy Number Three, the smart lad with whom Johnny had matched wits the day before.

"Hi, Eddie," Johnny greeted the bellboy.

"The name's Julius," retorted Bellboy Number Three and continued on his way.

Johnny shook his head. Julius was the last person he wanted to meet on this predatory expedition. The meeting might prove embarrassing in the long run.

He continued to his room, let himself in and shot the bolt on the inside. Then he took up a comfortable position in an easy chair and again opened the book on Tombstone. The volume accidentally opened in the back and Johnny discovered for the first time that it contained an index. And one of the first names that caught his eye was: *Walker, Jim. Page 211.*

Johnny turned to page 211. It was the beginning of Chapter Eighteen and bore the title: 'The Silver Tombstone.' Johnny shook his head in admiration — clever, these writers, making things so easy.

He began reading:

More fabulous even than Schiefelin's discovery was that of Jim Walker's Silver Tombstone Mine, near Hansonville. Walker was no miner, nor was he definitely connected with the Cowboy Gang which made its headquarters in Hansonville. He did, however, have friends in the gang, notably the notorious Jim Fargo and his source of livelihood was speculated upon. Walker was able to come to Tombstone frequently for convivial entertainment and always seemed to be well heeled with silver and gold — none of which he dug from the ground.

Perhaps the deadliest man in the entire Cowboy Gang, Jim Fargo, met his end under decidedly mysterious circumstances. Carrying a quart of whisky in each of the two pockets of his long bearskin coat, which he wore winter and summer, Fargo left Hansonville one morning for an unknown destination. This was not uncommon, for Fargo was known for his moody spells when he would have nothing to do with his associates. Fargo was believed to be the son of a wealthy doctor in California. It was known that Fargo upon these occasions betook himself to a hideout with a couple of books of poetry and a large quantity of liquor and read poetry and drank whisky until he was stupefied with both. When he recovered he would return to his regular haunts.

Fargo went upon his last reading and drinking orgy in October, 1883. He was gone for six days and then a Mexican found his body under a live oak tree. Two empty bottles were nearby, and Fargo had a bullet in his brain. One of his revolvers contained an empty cartridge. It was obviously suicide.

As his closest friend, Jim Walker took charge of the body of Jim Fargo. He dug a grave near the live oak tree — and discovered the Silver Tombstone Mine — a vein of silver that apexed two feet below the surface of the ground and at fifty feet depth grew to a vein forty feet wide. Walker eventually took three million dollars out of the Silver Tombstone . . .

There was more about the Silver Tombstone, but Johnny put down the book and reflected upon Jim Fargo. An outlaw and a killer, who read poetry; who was no good whatever upon earth but in dying gave the world a fortune.

Johnny sighed heavily and let the book rest upon his knees. Again it fell open at the index and he began to scan it. After a moment he exclaimed. The legend, *Tompkins, Dan, Page 117* had caught his attention. He turned to page 117 and found the reference to Tompkins, Dan.

> One of the original discoverers of the Apache Dance, Dan Tompkins sold his share for forty dollars and a pair of mangy mules.

Johnny chuckled. The descendant of the original Dan Tompkins had inherited a certain share of his ancestor's naïveté. Johnny looked for the name Ralston in the index, but could not find it. He tried Cotter, but drew a blank. Turning the page the name *Henderson, Milo*, caught his attention. He found the reference to Henderson on page 307. It read:

A former Apache scout, Milo Henderson came to Tombstone in the first weeks of its existence, established the weekly newspaper, *The Tombstone Lode* and when the town grew so that he was enabled to make it a daily, sold out and retired to the San Carlos Mountains to become one of the biggest ranchers in the state . . .

That was as far as Johnny was to read for some time. There was a soft tapping on the door. Johnny closed the book.

"Who is it?" he called peevishly.

"Helen Walker," came the quiet reply.

Johnny whistled softly and sprang to his feet. He started for the door, then realized that the book was in his hands. He looked around for a place to hide it and saw the sofa. Stepping to it he picked up one of the three cushions, put the book underneath and dropped the cushion back into place. Then he went to the door and unlocked it.

There was a worried expression on Helen Walker's face as she came into the room. "Surprised to see me?"

"A little," Johnny admitted. He pointed to a chair. "Won't you sit down?"

Helen Walker started for the chair, then detoured to the sofa. Johnny winced until Helen sat down on the cushion next to the one under which he had hidden the book.

"Decided to accept my offer for the Silver Tombstone?"

"No." Helen hesitated, then added, "Not yet."

Johnny seated himself in the big easy chair, facing her. The girl was primed; she had thought things over, was puzzled by his entry into the situation. And worried. So much so that she had been willing to swallow her pride and come to his hotel room . . . to pump him.

Johnny smiled and said nothing.

There was quiet for several seconds,

then Helen saw that if anyone was to talk it would have to be Helen. "Just who are you, Mr. Fletcher?"

"Johnny Fletcher."

"I know your name. Perhaps I should ask, *what* are you?"

"Just a guy trying to get along."

"The offer you made for the mine — that wasn't on your own behalf, was it?"

"No."

Helen Walker inhaled deeply, then exhaled slowly. "All right, Mr. Fletcher . . . "

"Johnny . . . "

Helen looked at him steadily and it seemed to him that there was more color in her features. "Johnny, then," she said. "I guess I've got to confide in you. I'm worried . . . "

"About what happened in San Bernardino?"

Her eyes tightened in sudden pain. "I wasn't in San Bernardino. I mean — I came through the town, naturally. You have to, driving from the east. But

I — I knew nothing about . . . that thing."

"Then what are you worried about?"

"Everything. I'm alone and everybody is opposed to me. My cousin, Tompkins . . . "

"I heard you last night." Johnny inclined his head toward the window.

She nodded. "They're trying to take the Silver Tombstone away from me."

Johnny looked at her thoughtfully a moment. "You suspect, of course, that the Silver Tombstone is a valuable mine?"

"That seems obvious. It's been shut down since 1886, but now suddenly everybody wants it. There can be only one reason. As a matter of fact, Tompkins admitted that he had discovered a rich vein of silver."

"Supposing he has and supposing he sits tight. I understand it would cost a fortune to explore the shafts and find his vein. Are you in a position to put the money into the mine?"

"I have an automobile," said Helen

Walker. "And something like two hundred dollars in cash. That's all."

"What has Charles Ralston got?"

"A friend in New York who'll back him for any amount. That's where Hugh Kitchen came in; he was the representative of Charles' friend . . . a man named Mainwaring, who owns a department store."

Johnny screwed up his mouth. "Then it looks bad — Ralston has the money; Tompkins knows where the silver is. You . . . "

"I own the Silver Tombstone."

"A hole in the ground. I read a book once in which there was a line that's always stuck in my mind. Something about, 'it takes a silver mine to run a silver mine.'"

Helen Walker leaned back wearily. At the same time her right hand dropped on the cushion beside her and she became aware that there was a bulky object under the cushion. It was the most natural thing in the world for her to raise the cushion.

She did — and found the book. The title registered instantly. "*Tombstone Days!*" she exclaimed. "Where did you get this?"

Johnny made a careless gesture, but Helen sat up and looked at him sharply. "This isn't . . . Charlie Ralston's?"

Johnny coughed lightly. "He loaned it to me."

"Then it was Charlie who sent you to me?"

"No," Johnny denied promptly, then winced as he realized that the denial narrowed the list of suspects down to one. Dan Tompkins. Helen saw it instantly.

"Tompkins!" she accused.

Johnny nodded.

"That simple-minded desert rat!" Helen exclaimed scornfully. "And he told you to offer three thousand for a mine that may be worth a million."

"*He* knows where the silver is," Johnny reminded her pointedly. "He told me that he spent two years poking around the innards of the

Silver Tombstone before he found the lode."

Helen got to her feet. "But if you're working for Tompkins how come you . . . ?" She held up the book.

"Ralston loaned it to me."

She gave him a strange look. "Do you mind if I don't believe that? As a matter of fact, Charles stole this book. It belonged to Uncle Jim. Right after one of Charles' last visits he was looking for the book and couldn't find it. He suspected Charles. Uncle Jim was greatly put out; he wanted *me* to have the book. Said it was one of a very few still in existence."

She put the book under her arm.

Johnny got up. "Wait a minute." He held out his hand. "I've got to return that book."

"It's mine!"

He shook his head. "Fight that out with Ralston — after I return the book."

"I'm not going to do any more fighting — with anyone."

Grimly Johnny advanced upon her. She retreated, then tried a quick flanking movement and headed for the door. Johnny dove after her, caught her about the waist. She whirled in his grasp, a fist doubled up. Johnny tried to duck, but took the punch on his cheekbone.

"Hey!" he exclaimed.

"Let me go!" she cried, struggling furiously.

It was the most natural thing in the world for Johnny to kiss her. She tried to hit him again and Johnny kissed her again. She stopped struggling.

After a moment Johnny released her.

"Okay?" he asked.

Her color was fourteen shades pinker. "I've got to go," she murmured.

Johnny slipped the book out from under her arm. "When will I see you again?"

"Call me — this evening."

He nodded and opened the door for her. After she had gone he stood for a moment, a thoughtful gleam in his eyes. Then he sighed, locked the door and went back to his chair. He opened the book and tried to find his place.

The panels of the door resounded to the rapping of knuckles.

"Open up, Fletcher!" cried the harsh voice of Tim O'Hanlon.

"Sold!" exclaimed Johnny, under his breath. "Sold by a dame." Aloud he exclaimed: "I'm not interested in making any horse bets."

"Still clowning, eh? Well, there's a man here'll do some clowning with you. He's from the police department . . . "

"Open up," a new voice.

Johnny groaned. He looked at the windows. It was ten feet across space to the room of Dan Tompkins. He was trapped. He got up and going to the door, unlocked it.

Tim O'Hanlon pushed into the room. He was followed by a heavy-set man of about forty.

"Lieutenant Meeker of the cops," O'Hanlon chortled.

Lieutenant Meeker took a folded

piece of paper from his pocket. He consulted it.

"You're the owner of a 1932 Ford Sedan, License No. 07A834?"

"No," said Johnny.

The detective frowned. "We'll go into that later. The night before last you stopped at a motel in San Bernardino . . . "

Johnny shook his head. "Wrong again."

"I can prove that," Meeker snapped.

"Go ahead."

Lieutenant Meeker stepped to the door of the bedroom, looked in, then turned back. "You have a friend named Sam Cragg . . . "

"Bingo!" exclaimed Johnny. "*That* time you win."

"All right, wise guy," said Meeker, showing his teeth. "We'll continue this down at the station . . . "

"You have a warrant?"

"I don't need a warrant for a murder charge."

Johnny held up his right hand, palm

to the detective. "Now, wa-ait a minute; fun's fun, but you can carry even fun too far. What's this about murder?"

"We'll talk about it at the station. The sheriff of San Bernardino County's on his way here."

"Still feel like clowning, Fletcher?" asked the house detective, who was enjoying himself immensely.

"Let's see," said Johnny, "you're in on this, too. Fine. I'll make you a co-defendant in my suit for false arrest."

"Okay," said O'Hanlon. "I'll give you something to really sue about." He walked up to Johnny, grinned wickedly and suddenly hit Johnny on the jaw.

Johnny went back, then recovered and started for O'Hanlon. Meeker caught hold of him. "Hold it!" the detective cried.

"Lemme at him, the big stiff!" Johnny yelled. "I'll pin his ears down for him."

Still struggling with Johnny, Lieutenant Meeker looked over his shoulder at

O'Hanlon. "You had no call to do that O'Hanlon."

"He's been asking for it," O'Hanlon retorted.

Johnny suddenly relaxed and the lieutenant let go of him. Johnny seated himself in the Morris chair. "All right," he said, "let's get this straight. Who'm I — supposed to have murdered?"

"A man named Kitchen," grunted Meeker. "But we'll go into it down at the station . . ."

"What about a lawyer?"

"You can call one after we book you . . . *if* we book you."

"Why can't I call one now?"

"Because it's against the rules." Meeker gestured impatiently. "Come on, let's get going . . ."

"He's stalling," exclaimed O'Hanlon. "He's expecting that fat friend of his."

Meeker scowled. "On your feet, Fletcher."

Johnny sighed wearily, and put *Tombstone Days* under his arm. "All right, fellows, I guess you've got me."

Meeker took his arm. "I could use cuffs . . . "

"Never mind, I'll go quietly."

They left the room and went to the elevator, where O'Hanlon pushed a button. The indicator showed that a car was already coming up. It stopped on the fifth floor and the door opened.

Sam Cragg was the sole occupant of the elevator. He blinked as he saw Johnny between the two detectives.

"Cops!" cried Johnny.

"That's his pal!" yelled O'Hanlon.

9

JOHNNY FLETCHER promptly dropped to his knees between the two detectives. Sam Cragg lunged forward, his powerful arms held out. They swept the two detectives together, cracking their heads. Then Sam slammed them back violently. Both men hit the wall on the far side of the hall. Johnny, meanwhile, scuttled into the elevator. "Come on, Sam!" he cried.

Sam leaped back into the elevator. Lieutenant Meeker was struggling to get out his gun.

"Down!" yelled Johnny to the elevator operator. The boy, however, was paralyzed with fright and Johnny shoved him aside. He slammed the lever forward, as far it would go. The car plummeted downwards. Johnny kept the lever depressed until they reached the first floor, then began to ease up on it. Even so the car overshot the basement by a few inches and he had to bring it back.

"Let's go," he shouted to Sam and led the way into the basement. Sam followed willingly enough and they skidded past the boiler room toward a metal-sheathed door at the far end. Johnny had a little trouble getting it open, but then they were outside, in the alley behind the hotel.

Without pausing in his stride, Johnny hit a stone wall across the alley, clambered up, then turned to help Sam, who wasn't too good at the climbing stuff.

"Alley oop!"

Sam gained the top of the wall, fell over into the yard beyond. Johnny dropped down and they rushed at top speed through a small yard, down a narrow walk and to the street beyond. A stout woman shaking out a rug on the pack porch looked at them in astonishment.

"Well!" she gasped.

"It ain't well at all, lady," Johnny replied.

"Take it easy, Johnny," Sam panted as they reached the street.

"They don't hang you in California," Johnny retorted. "They gas you."

They started across the street, entered another yard, cut through and came out on a street that was two blocks from the front of the hotel. Only then did they slow to a fast walk.

A bus was just pulling up at the corner. Johnny nodded to Sam and they made it by sprinting the last few yards.

Ten minutes later they got off the bus at La Brea and Wilshire.

Sam Cragg surveyed the busy intersection with an air of bewildered helplessness. "All right," he finally said, "we lost the cops, but how long can we keep away from them? Night's coming on; we can't walk the streets and we dassn't go to a hotel."

"Somebody snitched," said Johnny. "Somebody snitched to the flatfoot and

I'm going to find out who it was."

Sam grabbed Johnny's arm. "What difference does it make, Johnny? I've been thinking — I don't think I like gas. Let's get out of town. I've changed my mind about California. I don't like it."

"I'm beginning to like it less every minute, myself, Sam. But we're behind the eight-ball. I don't even know if we can leave town . . . You and your astrology."

"It ain't astrology, Johnny — you can't blame the stars for what's happening to us."

"Why not? Doesn't your book tell you that everything is written in the stars at the moment you're born . . . "

"No-no," exclaimed Sam. "It don't say anything of the kind. It says that you can be guided by the stars. You know what they mean, you know what to do . . . "

"I know what *I'm* going to do," said Johnny grimly. "Look over there, across the street . . . "

"Where?" asked Sam, looking;,

"That sign — Princess Astra . . . "

Sam scowled. "Cut it out, Johnny, that's a fortune teller's joint. You know what I think of fortune tellers."

"You're entitled to your opinion, Sam; I'm entitled to mine. Your astrology's let you down — I'm going to take a peek into the future. Come on . . . "

"I won't go in," protested Sam, as he followed Johnny across the street.

"All right, then wait outside."

But when they reached the two-story building, Sam followed Johnny up a dingy flight of stairs. At the top was a tiny waiting room, hung with velvet drapes on which were sewed silver stars.

A woman with straight black hair, tied in a knot, sat at a desk playing solitaire.

"Princess Astra?" Johnny asked.

The woman shook her head. "Princess Astra is meditating."

"How much would she charge to do

a little meditating for me?"

The woman sized up Johnny Fletcher. "Five dollars."

"That's a lot of dough," Johnny said. "There's a lady over on Sunset Boulevard tells your fortune for a buck."

"Princess Astra is *not* a fortune teller," said the woman with the black hair.

From behind the velvet curtains suddenly came a wheezy voice. "Who is it, dearie?"

"A customer," chuckled Johnny Fletcher. "A two-dollar one."

The curtains parted, revealing Princess Astra. She weighed about two hundred on the hoof, had a short fat neck and a mannish haircut. She wore a black tent for a dress.

"Which one of you's the comic?" she demanded.

"I want my fortune told," Johnny said. "But I only want two dollars worth."

Princess Astra regarded Johnny

through eyes that appeared as mere slits in her fat face. "You couldn't be a cop, because a cop wouldn't come right out and say he wanted his fortune told. We don't tell fortunes, you know. We give spiritual guidance. But what's this two-dollar nonsense?"

"Do you read horoscopes?" Sam asked.

The princess gave Sam a scornful look. "*That* bunk!"

Sam bristled. "Whaddya mean, bunk?"

"You heard me." She gestured beyond the curtains. "Come in."

Sam scowled, but followed Johnny and the princess to a large, square room that was hung with draperies. In the center of the room was a small table on which stood a crystal ball.

Princess Astra seated herself behind the table and motioned for Johnny and Sam to pull up chairs.

"Now, let's have your five dollars — each of you."

"Two for five," Johnny said.

The princess tapped the crystal ball with a beringed hand. "I don't have to look into this to tell that you're a cheap skate."

Johnny chuckled. Then he took out his roll and carelessly peeled off a five dollar bill. He allowed the princess to catch a glimpse of a fifty.

"Would you be interested in a complete reading?" the princess asked. "Past, present and future." She coughed. "For twenty-five dollars."

Johnny shook his head. "The sample five-dollar one will do." Then he pursed up his lips thoughtfully. "What do you do for twenty-five bucks? I mean, could you pull off a regular seance with horns and manifestations and such?"

The princess gave Johnny a thoughtful look. "You been readin' a book, dearie."

"Not lately. But I've got twenty-five bucks for a regular show, with, ah, the right answers for a friend of mine."

"All right," said Princess Astra. "Now, we've got the cards on the

131

table. Just what do you want?"

"I want to ask a man some questions . . . and give him some answers."

The princess patted the crystal ball. "Bring your friend here and I'll give him the god-damndest answers he ever heard."

"There may be a little trouble getting him here."

"What's his name? Where's he live?"

"His name's Dan Tompkins and he's staying at the Fremont hotel. He's a desert rat, from Arizona."

The princess got up heavily. "Say no more."

She started for the anteroom. Sam looked at Johnny in bewilderment. "Johnny," he whispered, "it won't work."

Johnny shook his head. "Shh!" He followed the princess out to the other room.

"Dearie," said Princess Astra to her receptionist, "get me Dan Tompkins at the Fremont hotel."

The woman with the tight black hair

began making the phone call. After a moment she handed the instrument to Princess Astra. Then Johnny whispered in the princess' ear, "Mention the Silver Tombstone."

The princess nodded and spoke into the phone. Her voice was suddenly hushed and dramatic. "Mr. Tompkins, this is the Princess Astra welcoming you to Los Angeles. You probably don't even know it, but you are here because I summoned you . . . Yes, while you were wandering out there in the vast reaches of the desert, I communicated with you the Silver Tombstone . . . what's that? . . . what's that? . . . You'll be here? In a half hour . . . The Princess Astra, on Wilshire, near La Brea . . . In a half hour, then . . . "

She hung up. "The man positively drooled," she told Johnny Fletcher. Then she sighed. "Why can't *I* get customers like that up here?"

"You're getting him."

"I meant on my own." Then a gleam came into her eyes. Johnny chuckled.

"You can have him, all for your own, after tonight."

"I'll give him such a show that he'll be afraid to eat breakfast without consulting me first." She swished aside the drapes. "Now, come in and tell me what you want from him."

Johnny was still telling the princess when a light flashed on the table beside the crystal ball. The princess exclaimed. "My goodness, he's here already." She hurried to the left wall and sweeping aside the drapes revealed a small door. "Get inside there. You can leave the door open when the drapes are in place."

Johnny and Sam crowded into a room that was no more than a closet and devoid of furniture.

"I don't like this," complained Sam. "It's a dirty trick."

"So's murder . . . Shhh."

From the seance room came the rumble of Dan Tompkins' voice . . . and the voice of someone else. Johnny reached for the drapes, parted them

134

slightly so he could look into the room.

Dan Tompkins was just seating himself beside Laura Henderson. There was an eager expression on Tompkins' face which was absent from that of the girl. In fact, Laura seemed quite dubious about the whole thing.

"I'll be frank," Laura said bluntly to the princess. "I don't believe in psychic phenomena."

"Neither do I," Astra retorted. "I don't believe in *any* of the hocus-pocus that spiritualists go in for. You show me a medium that resorts to table lifting and horns blowing in the dark and I'll show you a fraud."

"Then what *do* you do?"

"Nothing. You ask me questions and I give you answers — that's all."

"What sort of answers?" cut in Dan Tompkins eagerly.

"How do *I* know? I say what comes into my mind — that's all. Whether the answers are the right ones or not, I don't know."

Laura sniffed. "You see, Mr. Tompkins."

Even Old Dan was beginning to lose his enthusiasm. "If I'm going to spend good money . . . " Then a shrewd look came into his eyes. "How'd you get my name?"

The princess shrugged. "How should I know? I was sitting here, doing nothing, when all of a sudden your name popped into my mind . . . "

"But how'd it pop into your mind — if you didn't know my name?"

"Let's not go back over that," the princess said, tartly. "I told you I don't know how I know things. I just know, that's all. Some people think it's a gift. I, frankly, don't know." She made an impatient gesture. "Go ahead ask your questions and see if the answers suit you."

"All right." Tompkins hesitated, then shot out: "What's the Silver Tombstone?"

"Don't you know yourself?" the princess shot back.

136

"Of course I know. I'm asking you, though."

"Testing me, eh? Well — the Silver Tombstone is a mine. A silver mine in Arizona."

Tompkins grunted. "Who owns it?"

"*You'd* like to own it. But the real owner is a . . . a woman. Her name doesn't register clearly in my mind. It's something like Ellen . . . no, Helen."

Dan Tompkins was all interest now. "That's right." He shot a triumphant glance at the still skeptical Laura Henderson.

"Let *me* ask you a question," Laura Henderson said, suddenly.

"Go right ahead, dearie."

"What's my name?"

The princess almost choked. "Why, don't you know, dearie?"

"I know, all right, but I'd like to have you tell me."

Princess Astra gazed into her crystal ball. Johnny had coached her, given her the names of several people, but there had been two women's names.

And the princess had neglected to ask the name of Dan Tompkins' consort upon arrival. So she had to guess now — and the wrong guess would end the seance right then and there. Her brain worked rapidly; Helen Walker had been described as the owner of the Silver Tombstone, a self-possessed, independent type of girl. Laura Henderson, she had been told, was gay, a bit on the forward side.

This girl was certainly self-possessed . . . and suspicious. You could call her independent. That would be Helen Walker. Yet . . . would Dan Tompkins, who was trying to get the Silver Tombstone from Helen Walker, bring her here?

The princess didn't know. Silently, she cursed Johnny Fletcher. All this for a measly twenty-five . . .

"Walker," she said, suddenly to Dan Tompkins. "That's the girl's name — the one who owns the Silver Tombstone . . . " There was a slight narrowing of the old desert rat's eye — a touch of doubt and suspicion and Astra whirled toward Laura Henderson.

"And you, of course," she said smoothly, "are Laura Henderson."

She had won.

"All right," conceded Laura. "Now, just one more question . . . where is Johnny Fletcher?"

Behind the drapes, Sam Cragg winced. Johnny poked him in the ribs with his elbow.

At the seance table, the Princess Astra smiled blandly. "Who?"

"Johnny Fletcher."

"Oh, him," said the princess. She looked into her ball. "I see a small room — a hotel room. Johnny Fletcher is stretched out on the bed. He is sleeping."

"Where's the hotel room?" Laura persisted.

"The Fremont Hotel . . . "

"No," said Laura. "He isn't there — not now."

"Oh, but he is."

"Not any more. He ran out — with the police after him."

"The police?" A sharp note came into Astra's tone.

"Didn't you know?"

"Of course I knew." But there was a scowl on the princess' face.

"That's one of the things I want to ask you about," said Dan Tompkins. "As a matter of fact, I sized up this Fletcher as a pretty shrewd bird. A hard customer to get the best of. So when I heard about this, uh, trouble, I got to figuring. Somebody put the finger on him . . . Who was it?"

Again the princess had to guess. Tompkins was asking the question. He seemed anxious for an answer. So that eliminated him. Which left Joe Cotter, Charles Ralston — and Mike Henderson, to take in all of the men's names Johnny had given her. Since Tompkins couldn't immediately prove her wrong, she could guess fairly safe.

"Charles Ralston."

Dan Tompkins exclaimed. "The

dirty rat! So he's afraid of me."

"Yes," said the princess, taking it up from there. "He is in deathly fear of you. At this very moment he is cringing . . . lest you learn his secret . . . "

"What secret?" asked Tompkins eagerly.

" . . . The secret of the Silver Tombstone."

10

DAN TOMPKINS shoved back his chair. His eyes went quickly to Laura's face. Then he moistened his lips with his tongue. "Uh, yeah, what I was going to ask you was, do you think Helen Walker is likely to, ah . . . "

"What's the secret of the Silver Tombstone?" Laura Henderson suddenly cut in.

Astra passed a hand over her crystal ball, as if wiping away a mist. She peered into its murky depths, peered long and painfully, then she pressed a hand to her forehead.

"I can't tell you," she said and Dan Tompkins could not stifle an audible sigh of relief. "I can't tell you, because it would not be right . . . yet." She brushed the ball again. "The crystal is clouded . . . I see trouble . . . police . . . " She let out a low moan. "This man, Fletcher."

"Never mind Fletcher!" exclaimed Tompkins. "Tell me about myself . . . "

"You're mixed up with Fletcher. The police . . . "

"All right," snapped Laura Henderson. "What about the police? Are they going to nab Fletcher? Did he commit the murder . . . "

"Murder?" the princess gasped. "What's this about murder?"

Behind the velvet screen Johnny Fletcher cursed under his breath.

"What's the matter?" Laura asked witheringly. "Didn't your ball tell you about the murder?"

"I don't mix in murder." Princess Astra grabbed the edge of the table, pressed a button.

The black-haired secretary popped into the seance room. "Yes, Princess?"

"Call the police," said the princess. "Tell them — "

Johnny Fletcher jerked aside the velvet drapes. "Never mind," he snarled.

143

"Fletcher!" cried Dan Tompkins. "What are you doing here?"

"Being taken by a double-crosser . . . "

"Nadine!" said the princess sharply.

The secretary started to turn back, but Johnny Fletcher took two quick strides and cut her off. "Uh-uh," he said. Then, to the princess, "Give me back my twenty-five bucks."

"Go to hell," said her highness. "You didn't tell me anything about a murder. You just wanted some questions . . . "

"Say," cut in Tompkins, "I don't like this. I don't like it at all. What's the gag, Fletcher? Did you rig this up . . . ?"

"Of course he did," said Laura Henderson. "That's how she knew our names and that business about the Silver Tombstone."

"Fortune tellers," sneered Sam Cragg. "Anybody who'd believe in fortune tellers . . . "

Dan Tompkins blushed. "Fellas, I played fair with you. I paid you the dough you asked . . . "

"You got gypped," said Laura.

"Look, beautiful," Johnny Fletcher said, through bared teeth, "I like you a lot, but you keep on sticking that knife into me and you're going to spoil what might have become a beautiful friendship."

"I'm sorry about that," Laura retorted coolly. "And if there was any chance of that friendship materializing I'd be with you ... but you can't expect me to wait thirty-five years for you, now can you? And that's how long you're going to be in San Quentin ... if you're lucky enough to escape ... " She pantomimed an execution, by running a finger across her tanned throat.

"Come on, Johnny," said Sam, uncomfortably.

"All right, I'm going," Johnny said, bitterly. "But I'm not quitting. Somebody who's mixed up in the Silver Tombstone killed Hugh Kitchen and I'm going to find out who that someone is."

"I don't monkey with the cops," the

Princess Astra stated. "In my position I can't afford to. I'm going to report this . . . "

"Then give me back my twenty-five bucks."

"I'll give back nothing," Astra declared. "I earned that dough and I'm going to keep it."

Dan Tompkins got up suddenly. He made a movement toward his coat, but Sam Cragg held up a hand warningly. Tompkins' hand stopped in mid-air as he remembered what Sam had done to him that morning when he had pulled out a gun. He said, surlily: "This finishes our deal, Fletcher. You ain't working for me any more."

Johnny gave him a bitter look, then brushed past the receptionist, Nadine. At the door he turned. "Good-bye, now. But don't forget me. I'll be back." He went out. Sam Cragg gave Dan Tompkins one last scowl, then followed Johnny out of the seance room and down to the street.

Outside they walked quickly for a

block up Wilshire Boulevard. Then Johnny slackened his speed.

"*That* was twenty-five bucks wasted."

"What you expected to get out of a fortune teller I don't know . . . "

Johnny shook his head. "Dan Tompkins hasn't told us half of what he knows. They were fighting last night across from my room. Joe Cotter, Charles Ralston and Helen Walker." He frowned. "And I can't figure out where the Hendersons come in."

He took *Tombstone Days*, from under his arm and looked at it. For the first time Sam seemed to notice the book. "You snitched it."

"I was reading and the phone rang, so I figured I'd borrow the book and read it in my own room. Then the cop came along . . . You know, there's some interesting things in here; about old Jim Walker and Dan Tompkins — not our Dan, though. His father or grandfather . . . Wish I could get a chance to read the book all the way through."

"If the cops catch us you'll have a lot of time to read."

Johnny groaned. "This is no good. We've got to get out of town. And we can't go by train or bus, because the cops'll be watching the depots and bus stations."

"You mean we've got to hoof it," Sam said bitterly. "The doggone city limits of this town reach out thirty-five miles . . . "

"And after that, there's three hundred miles of desert." Johnny fixed his eye on a used car lot a short distance away. "No, we've got to have a car. A good one, too."

Sam grunted. "What sort of a car can you buy for around fifty bucks? We haven't got much more than that left, have we?"

"No, but we could buy a pretty good car for about two-fifty down."

"Yes," said Sam, sarcastically, "if we had two-fifty for the down . . . "

"There are ways . . . "

Sam blinked. "Johnny, you aren't . . . "

148

Then as he saw the speculative, gleam in Johnny's eyes, "Here we go again . . ."

"They're after us for murder," said Johnny. "Anything less is a breeze. Come along . . ."

He headed into the used car lot and began examining the cars. A man came out of a little building in the rear and strolled over.

"I'd like to get a jalopy," said Johnny. "Just about the worst jalopy you could imagine."

The salesman looked at him curiously. "Something to drive, or just to wear on your watch chain?"

Johnny grinned. "If it would run two-three miles, that'd be swell."

The salesman hesitated, eyeing Johnny skeptically. "Come along," he said, then.

Johnny and Sam followed him to the rear of the little building, where stood a late '20 Model T. "Look," said the salesman, "it's even got tires."

"Will it run?"

"We guarantee it unconditionally . . . that it'll run off this lot."

"Ten bucks," said Johnny.

"The junk man offered forty."

"I'll make it thirty."

"Thirty-five and it's a deal."

"All right, but you've got to give me papers."

"It's a deal."

Ten minutes later Johnny was behind the wheel and Sam beside him. He tried the starter. Nothing happened Johnny waggled a finger. "Your guarantee, Mister."

The salesman scowled and got the crank out of the rear of the car. He put it into a hole at the front of the machine, turned and turned and after a long time coaxed some response. The flivver began shaking and Johnny let in the clutch.

"S' long, Mister!" he cried to the salesman.

"Remember," said the salesman, "when you hit the street, you're on your own."

Johnny drove out of the lot and stopped the car a block away. But he did not shut off the motor.

"All right, Sam," he said, "give me three minutes, then drive into the place up there in the next block. You want two-fifty for her, but you'll come down to two hundred. Not a nickel less . . . "

"Are you crazy, Johnny?" Sam cried.

"If it doesn't work — yes. If it works, no. Leave it all to me. Act natural — you're a rube; you want two hundred for her and you don't give a damn. When you get the money, walk right back here and wait for me. You can't miss . . . "

"What do you mean, I can't miss?" wailed Sam, as Johnny walked off. He tried blowing the horn as Johnny refused to turn, but the horn wouldn't work. In despair he slumped over the wheel.

Johnny meanwhile strolled blithely up the street and turned into the big used car lot — a place more than twice the size of the one where they had purchased the flivver.

They were high-pressure boys here; two or three salesmen were coursing about the lot, waiting for victims. Two of them surrounded Johnny promptly.

"This Buick here," one of them cried. "Less than five thousand local miles; a steal at twelve ninety-five."

"Nope," said Johnny. "She's too low down on the ground."

"That's the beauty of a Buick," said the second salesman. "Holds the road . . . "

"No good for the desert, though. You got to have a car that's got some space underneath — even when you deflate the tires to about fifteen pounds of pressure . . . that's the only way to ride the sand, you know . . . "

"Here's a Packard that rides pretty high. But she's fifteen-fifty . . . "

"I'm not worried about the price," said Johnny. "Although I'd just as soon have an old car. When the wind blows the sand out there, your paint job goes pretty quick. And the ore doesn't help it much, either. Pretty rough stuff . . . "

"Ore," said the first salesman. "Mining man?"

Johnny nodded. "Got the best little tungsten mine in Mendocino County. That's where I'll be driving this car . . . if you can fix me up with what I want . . . something like that old-timer over there . . . " He pointed to the jalopy that Sam Cragg had just driven into the lot. "Those old boats are the thing for the desert . . . That doesn't happen to be your car, does it?"

The salesmen exchanged glances. One of them nodded almost imperceptibly and suddenly turned away. The other blocked Johnny's sight.

"Got a honey of an old Model A back here — an old doctor had it, but he wasn't practicing any more and he had the bus in his garage for seven years. Took it out every spring for a day, then put it back in the garage

153

again. She's as good as new . . . and only four-fifty."

Johnny looked at the shellacked old wonder. He shook his head. "I dunno; she's still not as high off the ground as I want." He walked around the car, kicked a tire, stooped and peered underneath.

The salesman frowned. "I'll be back in just a moment."

Johnny nodded absent-mindedly and started walking around the Model A again.

The second salesman strode quickly up to Sam Cragg's car, where the first salesman was leaning over the side. He turned as his fellow worker came up.

"A comic," he said, "wants two-fifty."

"Two-fifty," cried the second salesman. "Why, it's nothing but a pile of tin and rubber."

"Two-fifty," said Sam, doggedly. "Wouldn't sell if I didn't need a new plough."

"Look, Mister," said the first salesman, "we almost never buy a car as old as

154

this. In fact, there ought to be a law condemning such clap-trap, but you look like a nice fellow and we'll help you buy that plough. Fifty bucks — cash."

Johnny Fletcher started to come toward the group. The second salesman tried to head him off, but Johnny stepped aside and admired the old flivver.

"That's what you need for the desert. Doggone old cars are worth two of these city buses. Like to make you . . . "

"Just a minute," said the salesman, taking Johnny's arm. He started leading him away. "That's my wife's second cousin; got a big ranch out here in the Valley. Eighty-five acres of oranges, twenty lemon. You wouldn't think to look at him he was worth a half million, would you?"

"Him?" exclaimed Johnny. "Doesn't look like he'd have ten bucks to his name."

"That's his trouble," said the salesman. "Eccentric, been trying to get him to trade in that old — that little car for a Cadillac. Think he'd do it? No."

"Don't blame him, if he lives out in the desert. That's the kind of job you want . . . "

"But he doesn't live in the desert. He's attached to the car, that's all. Mm, he likes money pretty well. Ha-ha! Like all the rich guys, more they have, more they want. Maybe . . . if we offered him enough, he might sell that car." Brightening, "Then I could sell him a Cadillac."

"That's right," said Johnny. "What do you think he'll take for it?"

"He's asking four-fifty. Of course the car isn't worth it, but he doesn't want to sell. That's the trouble."

"Mmm," said Johnny. "I guess he *doesn't* want to sell." He shook his head. "Been to four lots already, though. That's the kind of a job I want for the desert. Suppose he'd take two and a half?"

The salesman shook his head. "Sure,

he wouldn't. I offered him three-fifty on a trade-in."

"I might go three hundred . . . "

The salesman could not conceal the gleam in his eye. "Wait here a minute."

Johnny nodded lackadaisically. The salesman hurried back to the other man, signaled him to one side and got into a whispered huddle.

The first salesman said: "The damn farmer's nuts. Holding out for two twenty-five."

Second salesman: "The other guy'll go three-fifty; I'm sure of it. Let's try him at two hundred."

"The heap's junk, I tell you," protested the first salesman. "He's got baling wire holding it together."

"A profit's a profit," said the second man.

They converged back upon Sam. "One seventy-five," said the first salesman.

"Two'n a quarter," persisted Sam.

"Two hundred!" cried the second salesman.

"Cash," said Sam.

He got out of the car and the first salesman grabbed his arm and hurried him toward the office. The other man detoured back to Johnny.

"He said he'd sell for three-fifty, but he's not too keen . . . "

"Well, I dunno," said Johnny. "I been thinkin' it over. I might go two-fifty . . . "

The salesman shot a look toward the office, into which Sam was just disappearing with the other salesman.

"I'd like to try him with three hundred."

Johnny hesitated. "Ask him."

Again Johnny was left alone, while the salesman hurried into the office, where Sam was already seated at a desk, signing a form. The second salesman nodded to the first, turned on his heel and went out of the office, back to Johnny.

"It's a deal."

"All right," said Johnny. "I suppose you throw in the registration and license transfer?"

"We don't usually, but we'll make an exception this time."

Johnny nodded and began strolling toward the flivver. He examined it critically, nodding approval as he stooped and looked under the car.

"She's all right," he said. He kicked a fender that was fastened to the body with wire. "Little wire won't hurt it."

"Of course not," said the salesman. "Shall we step into the office?"

"Just a minute," said Johnny. "The tires are kinda worn."

"There's plenty mileage in them yet."

"I dunno, the sand does things to tires . . . "

"You can get them recapped for five bucks apiece."

"Maybe so, but if I'm buying a car, naturally I want it in running condition."

"I'll guarantee there's a lot of miles in those tires," exclaimed the salesman. Sam Cragg was in the doorway of the office, shaking hands with the other salesman.

"You'll put it in writing?"

"Put what in writing?"

"The guarantee?"

"Yes!" cried the salesman, getting desperate. "I'll guarantee they'll go a thousand miles."

"Three thousand."

"All right, three thousand."

Sam Cragg passed behind Johnny and the salesman. The second salesman hovered in the background, then began coming forward. Johnny lifted up the hood, looked into the innards of the car, then let the hood fall back into place. Some rusty wire gave way and the hood fell askew. But Johnny didn't mind. He walked around the car, leaned over and tried the horn. There was no sign.

"Hey!" cried Johnny. "The horn doesn't work."

"We'll fix it!" howled the salesman.

Johnny shook his head. "When a horn's gone on a car, the car's pretty well shot. Tires no good, baling wire all over, horn broken . . ." He grabbed the steering wheel and shook it. "Steering wheel loose, too. Nope, I'm afraid she's too far gone for me . . . "

"What do you mean?" cried the frantic salesman. "You said you wanted this car — you agreed to pay three hundred for it . . . "

"I assumed it was in good condition," Johnny said, coolly. "Naturally, I'm not going to pay good money for a pile of junk." He shook his head. "Better let your cousin keep her."

"You can't do that, you made us buy her for you . . . "

"*I* made you buy this car — for me?" Johnny stared at the two salesmen in amazement. "Now, *wa-ait* a minute. I said I was interested in a car like this. I didn't say I would *buy* it . . . "

The first salesman grabbed Johnny's arm. "What kind of a game do you call this?"

Johnny took the man's hand, knocked it off his arm. "Don't you lay a hand on me . . . "

"I'll do more than that," snarled the man, "If you don't buy this car . . . "

"That settles it," said Johnny. "I wouldn't do business with you people now, if . . . "

He broke off and started rapidly out of the lot.

The two salesmen stared after Johnny a moment, then at each other, then at Johnny's back again. "You . . . !" one of them called after Johnny.

Johnny continued quickly out of the lot.

11

SAM CRAGG was nowhere in sight, but when Johnny got down to the second block, Sam popped out of a doorway.

"I aged ten years, Johnny," he panted. "I'm getting too old for those things."

"So am I," said Johnny. "For a minute I thought I'd have to yell for you to come back. They were going to jump me. In their place, I'd have punched me in the nose. At least." Then suddenly Johnny grinned. "That makes it up a little for all the people *they've* gypped on deals."

He stepped to the edge of the sidewalk and looked up Wilshire Boulevard. "Ought to be another used car lot nearby . . ."

Sam Cragg cried out. "Not — again!"

Johnny grinned. "No — a straight

163

deal this time. The two hundred's for a down payment on a car that'll run."

Sam drew a deep breath. "All right, as long as you don't try to beat them out of the down payment."

Johnny put his tongue into his cheek. "There's probably a way of doing that, but I haven't got time to think it out. You can lick any problem, if you give it enough thought." He frowned. "Wish I had time to think over this Silver Tombstone business."

"Out on the desert," Sam said, hastily, "you'll have a lot of time for thinking."

Johnny nodded and they started walking down Wilshire Boulevard. Two blocks away they found a third used car lot and after some negotiations purchased a fair Chevrolet for five eighty-seven dollars and fifty cents — beaten down from seven ninety-five dollars. They also paid one seventy-five dollars on it, signing a finance company loan blank and promising to pay outrageous interest. Johnny, naturally, never expected to pay any interest — or principal, but he knew, too, that the finance company would inside of two months repossess the car . . . no matter where Johnny had it at the time. The arm of the finance company is a long one. It was a purely temporary deal, as Johnny saw it.

So there they were then, at around six in the afternoon, driving carefully down Wilshire, out Figueroa to Los Feliz, then cutting across to Glendale by side streets. They skirted Eagle Rock and detoured completely around Pasadena.

They returned to Highway 66 just beyond Acadia, but left it after four or five miles, cutting south to another arterial. They jockeyed along it for a few miles, then cut back to Highway 66 at Fontana.

It was dark by that time, but Sam got more nervous by the minute. "Say, isn't this the neighborhood . . . ?"

"Yes," said Johnny, shortly.

Sam howled. "This is the last place in the world I wanted to come."

"It's the least likely place they'll be looking for us."

"I read a piece once where a policeman says that a criminal always returns to the scene of his crime and you just have to wait there and grab him."

"That may be true, but we didn't actually commit a crime."

"We beat the motel out of a night's lodging."

"That wasn't really a crime; it was a necessity. What were we supposed to do — sleep in the car just because we didn't have the price of a room?"

Sam shuddered. "Let's get away from here. My skin's all goose pimples already."

Ahead were the bright lights of a city. "Johnny," Sam said, with increasing alarm, "that's San Bernardino. We want to go *away* from there."

"We will — after I have a little

chat with the lad who runs the El Toreador."

"The El Toreador!" gasped Sam.

"The El Toreador," said Johnny firmly.

Sam Cragg took a long look at Johnny Fletcher, then slumped down in the seat beside him with the air of a man who has resigned himself to the inevitable.

And so Johnny drove carefully through San Bernardino and into the grounds of the El Toreador Motel. He stopped the car before the little office and climbed out. After a moment's hesitation Sam followed.

They met the manager in the doorway of the office.

"A nice cabin for the night?" the man asked.

"No," said Johnny. "We just stopped in to have a little chat with you."

Then the man recognized them. "Hey, you're the fellows were here the other night, the ones who . . . "

"Who — what?" Johnny asked harshly.

The man swallowed hard. "Why, uh, the ones who left here without paying for the cabin."

"How much was it?"

"Th-three dollars."

Johnny took out three dollars and handed them to the man. "You were still sleeping when we left in the morning."

The motel man crumbled the bills in his fist, moistened his lips with his tongue and backed up against his desk.

"You, uh, won't be wantin' to stay here tonight, will you?"

"No." said Johnny. "Sit down. You're making me nervous."

The man sat down promptly. But if he was making Johnny nervous, Johnny was making the man positively hysterical.

"All right," said Johnny. "Now, let's have some answers. How did the police happen to tie us up to this place? They found our car in an orange grove beyond Fontana . . ."

"They tricked me!" cried the motel

man. "They came around asking if some people who had a car with your license number had stopped here and I — I told them, yes; that you had jumped, I mean, forgotten to pay your bill. They didn't say anything about a dead man . . . not until they had found out."

Johnny nodded. He knew something of the ways of police. "What about Kitchen? *He* was registered here, wasn't he?"

The man shook his head violently. "No. And I never saw him in all my life."

"He wasn't registered here?"

"Absolutely not!"

"Mind letting me see your register?"

Eagerly the motel man grabbed up a ledger from the desk and turned back a couple of pages. "Here, see," he exclaimed. Then winced as he saw something on the page.

Johnny took the book and saw at once the entry that had caused the other to wince. It read: "No. 5, two

169

deadbeats. Watch them." He grunted and gave the man a withering look.

Then he ran his finger up the page. Cabin No. 14 had been rented to a Mr. and Mrs. Smith. Mr. and Mrs. Brown had occupied No. 7. Mr. and Mrs. Smith had used No. 1 and a Miss Smith No. 4.

"What's this Smith and Brown stuff?" he exclaimed.

The motel man cleared his throat. "Why, uh, I don't know. Only, well, we get four-five Smiths every night, it seems, besides a couple of Browns and Joneses."

Johnny got it, then. "What's your name — ?"

"Binney," said the motel man and looked apologetic about it.

Johnny stabbed at the book. "This Miss Smith in No. 4 — was she alone?"

"Sometimes they are and sometimes they aren't," Binney replied.

"Come again?"

"I mean, well, sometimes they register

170

alone, but in a little while there's a car drives in . . . visitors, you know. In this business . . . "

"Did Miss Smith have a visitor?"

Binney hesitated. "I really wasn't payin' any attention."

"You think she *did* have a visitor?"

"Y-yes . . . I think so."

"You didn't see him?"

"No."

"Then how do you know it was a him?"

Binney reddened. "I didn't. You put it into my mouth."

"It could have been a woman?"

"It could have been two people — three!" cried Binney. "I didn't pay any attention. In this business . . . "

"Yes, I know, it's tough. And it's full of Smiths. What about the guy in No. 6?"

Binney looked at Sam Cragg. "The big fellow who . . . " Sam Cragg growled.

"He signed his real name," Johnny said. "Joe Cotter."

"Yeah? What about him?"

"When did he leave?"

"He was gone when I got up."

"He didn't make any squawk about our car being gone?"

Binney's eyes squinted in pained recollection. "Say, how'd you work that?"

"Trade secret." Johnny tapped the register book a moment, then suddenly tore out the page.

Binney exclaimed, "Don't do that. I got to keep the record . . . "

"Somebody stole it," Johnny said drily. "Some deadbeat."

"The police will be after me about it," whined Binney. "It ain't right."

"It ain't right — that you turned us in." Johnny signaled to Sam. "Well, we've got to be going."

"Wait a minute," said Sam. "We can't leave here and let . . . " he nodded to Binney.

Johnny sighed. "I suppose you'll grab the phone and call the cops the minute we leave."

"Oh, no!"

Johnny nodded. "I believe you, but just the same . . . " He stepped to a closet door and opened it. Then he turned back to Binney. "Got a key for this?"

"I'll smother in there."

"There's a half inch crack under the door. You get your face down to it and you can stay there a week . . . We need a head start."

He held out his hand. Reluctantly Binney reached into his pocket and brought out a ring of keys. Johnny took the ring and herded Binney into the closet. He closed the door and locked it with one of the keys. Then he dropped the ring on the table.

Sam Cragg rapped tentatively on the door. "He'll break that down in two minutes."

"*You* might, but *he'll* need a half hour. Which is all the start we can expect."

Johnny started for the door, then caught sight of a road map tacked to the wall. He ripped it down, folded and stuffed it in his pocket. On his way out he picked up a flashlight lying on a stand.

Two minutes later, with Sam Cragg at the wheel, they were rolling out of San Bernardino. Leaving the lights of the city behind them Johnny took the road map from his pocket and turned the flashlight on it. He studied the map intently for a couple of minutes. Then he shook his head.

"There're two quick ways out of California from here," he said. "One, really, up to Barstow — the main drag. But at Barstow you can cut straight across Highway 66 to Needles, and Kingman in Arizona. It's the shorter, but tougher way. The other way is to take Highway 91 at Barstow, to Las Vegas, Boulder Dam and then to Kingman. It's a few miles longer than through Needles, but actually you can make better time, because the mountains aren't bad . . . A man'd be crazy to take any other road, if he was in a hurry to leave the state."

Sam Cragg scowled. "So?"

"So we're crazy. Binney'll get out of that closet in a few minutes. He'll call the cops and they'll telephone to Barstow. We might beat them through Barstow, but they'd get us somewhere along the stretch between Barstow and Las Vegas or Barstow and Needles." He sighed. "We got practically a tank full of gas and they don't know our license number — yet, so I guess we go up to Mojave, along Death Valley and into Nevada — about three hundred miles out of our way."

"The hard way," said Sam Cragg sarcastically. "Well, hold onto your hat."

12

AT six in the morning, Johnny Fletcher, who had been driving the last two hundred miles, braked the car to a stop in front of a restaurant and nudged Sam Cragg who was dozing fitfully beside him.

"Breakfast time!"

Sam Cragg groaned and opened his eyes. He twisted himself and winced as cramped muscles protested. "Are we still in California?" he asked.

"The sign says it's Tonapah, Nevada — but it looks just like all the other towns we passed through the last two hundred miles."

They got out of the car and went into the restaurant. It was a long narrow room with a counter running down one side and a row of slot machines down the other.

"Yeah," said Johnny, "it's Nevada."

He took a quarter from his pocket, dropped it into the nearest slot machine, pulled down the lever and continued on to a stool. The slot machine whirred, there was a click . . . and a stream of quarters poured down the slot into the cup. Two or three spilled overboard and hit the floor. Johnny was off the stool and in a single bound reached the slot machine.

He scooped out quarters, picked up the ones that had spilled on the floor. He began counting them. "Twenty quarters — five bucks," he announced after a moment to the dumbfounded Sam Cragg. "How long has this been going on?"

"It happens all the time," said the waiter behind the counter. "Somethin' wrong with that machine. Fella came in here yesterday, put in a quarter and hit the jackpot . . . Got seventy-four bucks."

Johnny was already putting a quarter into the machine.

Ten minutes later he climbed back

on the stool at the counter, a wiser, sadder man. He had fed back the twenty quarters, originally won, and another twelve dollars.

"When we get out of here," he said to Sam Cragg, "kick me where it hurts."

"I think you're wrong to quit now," Sam said. "The jackpot's just about full. The next quarter might tip it."

"Ahrrr!" He signaled to the waiter. "Let's have that coffee now."

"Sure," said the waiter. "Would you be interested in rolling the bones? The cook's going off duty in five minutes and he likes a game before he goes home." He grinned apologetically. "On account of the places are only open nights and he works at night and don't get a chance to gamble."

"Twelve bucks for a coffee is good enough for me," Johnny retorted. "As a matter of fact, I'm thinking of starting a petition to outlaw gambling in the state of Nevada."

"They do that," said the waiter, "and

178

we'll close up this place. What do you think we make our money on here?" He pointed at the slot machines.

He brought the coffee, so black and strong that the thin milk he set out did no more than lighten it two or three shades.

. . . At noon Johnny was swinging the Chevrolet around the beautiful grades just south of Boulder Dam. For twenty minutes it was like riding a roller coaster — up a steep grade, down, around a curve, then another. But suddenly the car rolled down the last grade and the black macadam road stretched ahead like a black ribbon down the straightest, flattest, longest stretch of road Johnny and Sam had ever seen — fifty-some miles, to Kingman. Now, Johnny really let out the Chevrolet — seventy-five miles an hour, eighty and even eighty-five.

The little car ate up the miles. By six o'clock they were in Phoenix. They had dinner at a small restaurant, then climbed into the car, turned on the headlights and started for Tucson.

At eleven-thirty Tuscon was behind them, but Johnny Fletcher was about ready to throw in the sponge. He had slept only fitfully the night before, during the times that Sam Cragg drove. He was even relieved therefore, when a clanking somewhere in the innards of the Chevrolet promised a forced halt to their journey. But it was ten minutes before they saw a light ahead and the clanking by that time had become serious.

He tooled the car into the little wayside filling station which showed a light.

He and Sam got out of the car and for a moment the car and the filling station seemed to swirl around him. Then his head cleared and he started for the door of the station. The light, he saw now, was not in the station itself, but in a room behind it.

He tried the door of the station and discovered it was locked. He rattled the doorknob, then pounded on the door.

The clamor produced no results.

Behind Johnny, Sam muttered under his breath. It sounded something like, "God-damn country."

"The country's all right," snarled Johnny. "It's the people in it." He took a deep breath and yelled suddenly: "Hey, wake up, inside!"

Sam began kicking at the door.

A figure finally appeared in the doorway of the room behind the station "Whaddya want?" it asked in a voice perfectly audible.

"Some service," Johnny yelled back.

The man inside shook his head. "Place is closed for the night."

"This is an emergency," Johnny cried. "Open up."

"Won't," was the reply. "Go 'way."

Sam Cragg picked up a rock and poised it in his hand. "Open up or I'll heave this through the window!" he threatened.

That produced results. The man inside switched on a light in the filling station and came to the door. He

181

opened it — and thrust out a revolver about fourteen inches long.

"You'll do what, Mister?" he asked coolly.

Johnny and Sam moved back three feet as if struck by lightning. Johnny grinned sickishly. "Take it easy!"

The man with the gun — a real ancient — showed a few blackened teeth. "A couple of tough hombres, eh?"

"Uh-uh, not me," said Sam Cragg, eying the big gun. "I was only joking."

"This place is all glass," said the old man. "I don't like people who throw stones — not with me living in a glass house. Catch on?"

"Sure," said Johnny. "But we're in trouble. Something's wrong with our car — "

"I own this place," said the old man. "But my mechanic does the work — and he quits at nine o'clock."

"Then we're stuck," said Johnny. "How far is it to the next town?"

"Plenty."

Johnny groaned. "Guess we'll have to take a chance." Sam nodded gloomily and they climbed back into the car. The old man came to the door and watched them.

Johnny stepped on the starter. Nothing happened. He tried again. There was still no response.

"Well," said Johnny, "that settles it. We sleep in the car."

"You can come inside," the old man offered, surprisingly enough.

Johnny and Sam climbed out of the car and followed the old man into the filling station. A lean man with walrus mustaches came out of the back room.

"Somethin' wrong with their car, Lafe," the old filling station proprietor said. "You can look at it in the morning."

Johnny exclaimed, "Is *he* your mechanic?"

"Yeah, sure," replied the old man.

"Then why can't he look at the car now?"

"'Cause it's after his working hours, that's why."

Lafe nodded agreement. "You probably need your valves ground, that's all."

Johnny gritted his teeth. "Look, folks, it's twelve o'clock at night; we're stuck here in the middle of the desert; I understand there isn' a town in miles — "

"Twenty-eight," said Lafe, laconically.

"All right," said Johnny, "twenty-eight miles. It's after working hours. So we'll pay you extra."

Lafe shook his head. "A man can only work so many hours a day. I'll grind your valves in the morning."

"They don't need grinding," exclaimed Johnny. "There's something broken — the motor won't start."

"Valves," insisted Lafe, "cost you thirty-two bucks."

"That's a holdup!" burst out Sam.

Lafe shrugged. The old man smacked his leg with the barrel of his long gun. "Why don't you try somewhere else?"

"Because the car won't start!" snapped Johnny. Then he sighed in sudden surrender. "All right — thirty-two bucks."

"In the morning," said Lafe. "Grinding valves is a big job."

"Maybe it isn't the valves. It *could* be something just wrong with the starter."

Lafe shook his head. Then he grinned. "It's the valves . . . on account of it's twenty-eight miles to the next town."

"Might as well come in and set," invited the oldster.

He went into the room behind the station. The others followed. Johnny noted that the place was fitted up as a combination kitchen and bedroom; at least it contained two bunks, a stove and a table. Scattered on the table was a pack of cards.

The old man gestured to the cards. "Me and Lafe was just finishing a rubber."

"A rubber?" Johnny asked.

"Yeah, we're playin' some newfangled game. Don't know much about it."

He seated himself at the table and Lafe went to the other side. He picked up the cards and dealt. Johnny looked at Sam, then shrugged and pulled up a chair to kibitz.

Lafe dealt clumsily. He played even worse and after eight or ten draws the old man went down with ten and caught Lafe with twenty-two points.

"That finishes the game," the oldster exulted. He began figuring the score. "You owe me eight forty-five," he said, after awhile.

Lafe grunted and produced the money. Johnny's eyes narrowed. "What're you playing for?"

"Two cents a point." The old man shook his head. "First time I've won in a week. Lafe doubles his pay."

"Mmm," said Johnny. " . . . I saw some fellows playing this game a few weeks ago. Looked interesting . . . "

"Like to try a rubber?"

Johnny, looking at Sam, saw the

latter wince. "For two cents a point? I'm not much of a gambler . . . "

"By the way," said the old man, "my name's Johnson — Luke Johnson . . . Tell you what I'll do. Your bill'll be thirty-two dollars tomorrow. I'll play you a rubber, double or nothing . . . "

Johnny pretended to hesitate, then finally nodded. "That's a bet."

Luke Johnson picked up the cards, squared them. "Low man deals."

He cut a deuce and Johnny a king.

Johnson dealt, even more clumsily than had Lafe awhile ago. Johnny picked up his hand, discovered that he had a pair of jacks and nothing else.

"Double for blitz, of course," said Johnson. "If you blitz me you get the work done for nothing and I give you thirty-two dollars, in addition."

"And if I lose?"

"Then you pay one twenty-eight."

Johnny swallowed hard and looked again at his hand. "All right," he said.

"I've got nine points," said Johnson,

putting down his hand.

Johnny cried out in consternation. "I didn't even get a chance to draw."

Johnson shrugged. "All luck, this game. Sheer luck . . . Let's see, you got forty, forty-eight, fifty-six, sixty-one points." He grinned wickedly. "Thirty-nine points more and I'm out."

"What?" cried Johnny. "We're playing three games across."

"Uh-uh. A game's a hundred points . . ."

"*Each* game," protested Johnny. "But we're playing three games — everybody plays three games."

"Never heard of it. A single game's all we ever play. Look — " he scooped up the score between himself and Lafe. "See?"

Johnny looked and didn't like it. Another lucky hand . . . and he would lose one hundred and twenty-eight dollars . . . more money than he and Sam had between them.

Lafe hitched up his chair beside Johnny. "This is gonna be good," he said, breathing down Johnny's neck.

Sam pulled up a chair beside old Johnson. He caught Johnny's eye and nodded significantly. The old man dealt the cards, spilling them once while shuffling. Johnny sorted out his hand: three treys, two fives, two kings, two queens and a ten. Not a bad hand if he connected.

He drew a jack and discarded it. Johnson picked it up and threw a five. Johnny scooped it up and discarded a ten.

"Gin," said Johnson.

"No!" howled Johnny.

"Yes," chuckled the old boy. He looked at the cards that Johnny dropped. "Forty points — and twenty for gin. That's sixty and a blitz. You owe me one twenty-eight . . . "

"For two hands . . . "

"Okay, Johnny," said Sam Cragg. His hand brushed against Luke Johnson's hip, grabbed the old Frontier model in the belt and whipped it out.

Johnson kicked back his chair and sprang to his feet. Sam slipped sidewards and waved the gun at first Johnson, then Lafe. "A thieves' den!" he cried.

"That gun ain't loaded," said Johnson calmly. He went to a wall telephone and took down the receiver.

"Get away from that phone!" Sam snapped.

Johnson began dialing. "Hello, Highway Patrol," he said.

"Get away!" Sam roared.

"This is Luke Johnson," Johnson said into the telephone. "There're a couple of stickup artists here . . . "

Sam averted the muzzle of the gun and pulled the trigger. A click was the only result. He howled in rage and threw the gun to the floor. Johnson said, "Excuse me a minute," into the phone, then reached to a shelf nearby. He whirled on Sam with a twin to the other Frontier model.

"*This* one is loaded," he said. He lowered the muzzle, pulled the trigger. A terrific explosion rocked the little room and splinters flew from the table. "See?"

Sam was already hurtling through the door into the filling station. Johnny knocked the table aside and followed. Old man Johnson calmly sent a bullet after Johnny.

Sam was whipping open the outer door when Johnny came through from the rear room, but so great was Johnny's speed, that he collided with Sam just outside the door.

13

OLD man Johnson came hobbling outside, but by *that* time Johnny and Sam were fifty yards from the filling station . . . and going fast. The old boy gave them an additional burst of speed by sending a couple of bullets winging over their heads.

It was every man for himself, and when Johnny pulled up a quarter of a mile from the filling station, Sam was a hundred yards behind. And having tough going. Johnny dropped to the ground and waited for Sam to come up.

"Jeez!" panted Sam, when he finally arrived.

"You can say that again," cried Johnny.

He looked back toward the filling station and discovered that he and

Sam had taken off across country, away from the highway. As a matter of fact they had even run up hill, for the filling station was some distance below them.

The moon was almost full and the station stood out brightly. Johnny got to his feet. "We've got to go back," he announced.

"Haven't you had enough?" Sam howled.

"I have — but they've got our car and we're lost without a car, out here on the desert . . . "

"We're lost if we go back," Sam protested. "He was calling the cops . . . "

"A bluff . . . "

"Yeah? Listen . . . !"

Johnny listened and the thing he heard sent a little shiver through him. A siren, still some distance away, but coming closer. He groaned. Far to the left, down the highway, a red light appeared.

"It's the cops, all right."

"Goddamit!" Sam Cragg cursed.

"Goddamit the hell!"

"Come on," said Johnny. "We're in no position to be picked up by cops — on any charge whatever."

The siren was still piercing the night and the red light on the highway was growing brighter.

"I can't run another step," Sam complained.

"I'll bet you can," said Johnny. "I'll bet you can run quite a ways . . . "

And Sam did. They reached the crest of the hill a few minutes later, by which time the red light had come up to the filling station. Johnny stopped a moment to look down and suddenly cried out, as the red light shot out across the desert and silhouetted him on the hillside.

That he was seen was quite obvious, for a bullet whined somewhere through the air and a moment later came the report of a gun — a much heavier, sharper report than that made by the old Frontier Model. A rifle.

They ran again, a quarter mile at

pretty good speed, then another quarter mile at a stumbling lope. Sam fell two or three times, but always picked himself up again. Then he fell and remained on the sand. Johnny came back to him, threw himself down beside Sam.

They remained on the ground for five minutes, then Johnny sat up.

"Think you can make it now?"

Sam rolled over on his back and looked up at the sky. "No," he replied.

Johnny did not urge him. But after awhile Sam got wearily to his feet. "All right."

Johnny rose. Without speaking they began plodding through the sand. It was tough going and they stopped to rest frequently. But they kept on. Sam knew as well as Johnny that they had to put as much distance as possible between themselves and the filling station on the highway.

There might not be a pursuit in the night, but in the morning there most certainly would be. And by morning they had to be pretty far away.

Dawn came early on the desert and in a little while the sun rose in the east, a great red ball. Johnny and Sam sat down and surveyed the landscape. The desert seemed to stretch out endlessly in every direction. In the north, far away, were white-crested mountains and there were mountains to the east. But between them was a vast stretch of wasteland.

"How far would you say we've traveled since Tucson?" Johnny asked.

Sam groaned. "I didn't pay any attention."

"Neither did I, but we were crowding it and we left Tucson about a quarter after eleven . . . It was right around twelve when we hit that filling station . . . Mmm, I'd say we were forty-fifty miles from Tucson then . . . Can't be so awfully far to Tombstone . . . "

"They may be putting up a tombstone for *us* out here," Sam said, bitterly, "if they ever find our bodies . . . "

"That's what they said to Ed

Schiefelin, the guy who discovered Tombstone."

"I wish the hell he'd never discovered it," complained Sam. He loosened his shirt collar. "It gets hot damn early out here on the desert."

Johnny looked steadily at Sam. "I read a book about Death Valley once . . . "

"Don't tell me about it!" Sam said, quickly. "Which way's civilization?"

"Tombstone ought to be east . . . and north. But we don't want to go north too much, because we'll hit the highway . . . " Johnny hesitated. "I think."

Sam looked at him sharply. "All right, let's travel."

They started in an easterly direction. The sun began to rise and inside of ten minutes both men were dripping with perspiration. They forgot their weariness and began traveling faster. Before eight in the morning Sam was in distress and Johnny not much more comfortable.

"We've got to have some water," Sam gasped.

"We'll have to head north," Johnny said. "I don't see any signs of life in the east at all."

Without a word Sam started northward. Johnny trudged at his side. Within a half hour Sam turned to Johnny. "What was that stuff about Death Valley?"

"It said you couldn't go more than a few hours in the desert without water. The heat dehydrates you . . . "

"You aren't sweating any more."

"Neither are you," said Johnny soberly.

Ten minutes later they labored up a sand dune and threw themselves on the top. They lay motionless for a few minutes, then Johnny stirred.

"It can't be more than a few miles more to the highway."

"If it was only a half mile, I couldn't make it."

"You've got to, Sam."

"You go alone — I'm all in."

"I'm as tired as you are, Sam," said Johnny. "But you just can't quit." He got to his feet, nudged Sam with his foot. Sam got to his knees, looked up and gritted his teeth.

Johnny reached down and helped his friend. They started off, keeping hold of one another. Their gait was stumbling and uneven, but their peril kept them going, to another sand dune, even higher than the previous one.

It was Johnny who gave out then. Sam stumbled halfway up the dune, stopped and saw Johnny on his knees down below. He turned and went back.

"Come on, kid," he said.

Johnny smiled weakly. "This does it, Sam."

Sam put his arms about Johnny, tried to raise him to his feet, but found that his great strength had gone.

"Let's make it to the top," he panted.

Johnny shook his head; the strength for it was about all he had. Sam turned, tried the dune once more, but was

199

down on his knees before he had gone a dozen feet. He slipped back through the deep sand.

Heat waves shimmered over the desert.

For a long time neither spoke. Then Johnny finally croaked. "So long, pal!"

Sam flopped a hand weakly in acknowledgment.

Minutes later, Johnny said, "Sam . . . that time in Louisville, when I beat the hotel out of six weeks' rent . . . I wish I hadn't done it . . . "

"What about the Hollenden in Miami?"

"We really didn't have any money that time, but in Louisville, I had a hundred dollar bill pinned to my sock . . . "

"Huh?" Sam sat up. "You never told me . . . "

"I know. I thought I had a good one at Churchill Downs and figured to get us back in the chips. I put the hundred on the nag's nose . . . It came in eighth."

"Dammit, Johnny!" cried Sam. Then, "Hey . . . !" He scrambled to his feet. "Look — Johnny!"

Johnny raised himself, saw Sam standing and got up himself. "I guess we can go a little farther, eh?"

"Let's go!"

They gained the top of the dune — and both cried out. An eighth of a mile below was a stream and beside the stream an Indian village; a populated village, consisting of twenty or more hogans.

Their fatigue fell away. They scrambled down the incline. They were a hundred yards from the village, when Johnny suddenly caught Sam's arm and stopped. He nodded toward the Indian encampment.

Some sort of a ceremony was about to be enacted. The Indians, forty or fifty of them, were gathered in a square at the edge of the water. They were bedecked in native finery, their faces smeared with paint. A drum began pounding, then another and another.

Several of the Indians began chanting.

"A war dance!" exclaimed Sam.

"Don't be silly. The Indians haven't been on the warpath in sixty years."

"Are you sure?"

Johnny nodded. But there was a little frown on his forehead. Again they started toward the Indian group — now a frenzied group of chanting, dancing and stamping Indians.

They approached unseen, for the Indians — even the women and children on the outskirts — were enthralled by the dance. They were thirty feet away, when a sudden break in the square revealed what was going on inside. Sam Cragg cried out in horror.

"He's got a snake in his mouth!"

Johnny had already seen. It was hard to believe, but it was true. One of the dancing Indians had a fat rattlesnake between his teeth; a live, squirming snake. On each side of the snake-biter, dancing Indians waved feathers to attract the snake's fangs. Even as

Johnny and Sam watched, the snake struck at a bundle of feathers.

Johnny nudged Sam and they began skirting the dancers, intending to reach the edge of the stream.

But it was too late. An Indian had spied them. He yelled suddenly and came for Johnny and Sam. There was a hissing snake in his fist.

"Yow!" cried Sam Cragg and jumped no less than six feet.

Johnny Fletcher stood his ground, although he was sure that the short hairs on the back of his head were standing up straight.

"Cut it out!" he exclaimed.

"Ai-yai-ai!" howled the Indian and thrust the snake's head toward Johnny's face.

Johnny ducked frantically and instinctively drove his fist into the Indian's mouth. The Indian gasped and went over backwards, the snake flying from his hand. It missed Johnny by not more than an inch, hit the ground and began squirming away.

The Indian scrambled to his feet. He was a young brave, hideously painted and his face distorted by rage. Johnny backed away.

"Sorry, old man," he said.

The Indian sprang at him. Johnny clinched with him, found that his strength had not yet returned and was borne backwards to the ground. Another Indian rushed in, pounced down and the two started to spread-eagle Johnny to the ground.

Then Sam Cragg came back. He reached down, took hold of each of the Indians and lifted them bodily off Johnny. Johnny scuttled out from underneath, got to his feet.

He looked past Sam Cragg, saw the entire Indian tribe swarming down on them.

"Let's go, Sam!" he yelled.

Sam let go of the Indians and sprinted for the creek. Johnny was at his heels and behind them the entire Indian tribe. They hit the water at full stride. Luckily it was only a few inches deep and did not impede their progress.

They reached the shore on the far side and kept going. The Indians, however, did not follow past the water, but piled up on their own side and threw stones after Johnny and Sam.

Johnny and Sam slackened their speed after a few moments, then began cutting diagonally back toward the water, when they saw that the Indians were not pursuing them.

They reached the stream three or four hundred yards from the Indian camp, dropped to their stomachs and dipped their faces into the water. It was quite cool and they drank deeply.

After a moment they got up and grinned at one another. "Fifteen minutes ago I thought I was a goner," said Sam.

Johnny chuckled. "That was when we didn't know there was any water nearby. I felt better the minute I saw the water."

Sam nodded toward the Indians. "That snake stuff . . . !" he shuddered.

14

FOLLOWING the stream, a half mile from the Indian village, Sam and Johnny came upon a little-traveled desert road. A weathered wooden sign on a sagging post read: *Tombstone, 8 miles*.

They took a last, long drink of water, then struck out toward Tombstone. It was surprising how quickly they had recovered from the dehydrating of the morning sun. A quart or so of water and they were almost as good as before. A little more tired, perhaps. But with the knowledge that their destination was only eight miles away and that they were on the right road, their fatigue fell away from them.

In a little more than two hours the desert road climbed a steep hill and at the top of it cut a paved highway. Shortly ahead was a sign: *Boothill*

Cemetery. Johnny and Sam walked over to it, read some inscriptions on the stones.

"Nobody here we know," Johnny commented.

"You didn't expect anyone, did you?"

Johnny shook his head. "Some of our people had grandfathers."

A short distance ahead and they were in Tombstone proper, a bleak, dying town that retained little of its onetime glory. A street or two of crumbling adobe and brick houses, a few stores; a couple of rundown motels that catered to a few tourists who wanted to spend a night in a once glorious boom town.

They turned into a drugstore and ordered a coke and a ham sandwich apiece. The soda jerk, a grizzled man of about fifty, sized them up, while they ate. "Like to buy some postcards?" he asked.

"Why?" Johnny asked.

"Great old town, Tombstone," was the reply. He pointed to the window.

"Right out there Buckskin Frank Leslie shot down Billy Claiborne. And over there, behind that building is the O.K. Corral, scene of the most celebrated gun fight of the Old West, the battle between the Earps and the McLowerys and the Clantons . . . "

"You seem pretty well posted on the old days."

The soda jerk shrugged. "Can't help it; tourists ask you questions. Been a lot of books written about Tombstone . . . "

"Ever hear of one called *Tombstone Days*?"

"No, but we got one here called just *Tombstone*. Cost you only . . . "

"Thanks," said Johnny, "but I'm thinking of writing a book about Tombstone myself and I'd rather not read any more books about it. Might confuse me. I'd like to talk to some old-timers, though — fellows who were here when it was all happening . . . "

"Man you want's Old Bill Sage. He slapped Curly Bill's face one time. He also took Wyatt Earp's gun away from him." The man behind the counter chuckled. "To hear him tell it."

"Liar, eh?"

"Sure, but he *was* here during the old days."

"Might be worth talking to. Where'll I find him?"

"Over on Tough Nut Street. Can't miss him. He'll be sitting out on the porch . . . white beard about a foot long."

"Thanks."

They left the drugstore and at the corner turned into Tough Nut Street. They had no difficulty finding Old Bill Sage, for he was, as the soda clerk had told them, seated in an ancient rocking chair, a full white beard covering his entire chest and bright, blue eyes taking in Johnny and Sam as they approached.

"Mr. Sage?" Johnny asked, as they came up.

"Bill Sage," the ancient replied. "You've come to see me about my mine, eh?"

"Why, no," Johnny said. "Just thought we'd stop by and talk about the old days . . . "

"What old days?"

"Why, the days when Tombstone was . . . "

Bill Sage spat out a stream of tobacco juice. "Trying to knock down the price, huh? Well, lemme tell you, It won't work. I've had a lot of experience with mine promoters in my time and you can't get away with it. I've been here since the beginning and I've seen them come and go . . . "

"I don't doubt it, but I only wanted to ask you . . . "

"Yeah," cut in the old man. "You're not interested in the price. You only want to run down Tombstone, call it a ghost town and such nonsense. Then when you get me all discouraged, you offer me about half what the mine's worth."

"I'm not interested in buying a mine," Johnny protested, "and I don't

210

give a damn if Tombstone is a ghost town today . . . "

"See!" cried Bill Sage triumphantly. He fixed his bright blue eyes on Sam Cragg. "You're one of the Hansonville cowboys . . . "

"Me?"

"Yes, you. I can spot you fellows a mile away. Call yourselves cowboys and you ain't nothin' more nor less than rustlers, that's what you are."

Sam Cragg caught Johnny's eye and gestured with his head, to indicate that they were wasting their time with a senile old coot. The old man caught the gesture, however, and sprang to his feet.

"I saw that!" he yelled. "I saw it and I ain't afraid of you. And that goes for Curly Bill and Jim Fargo, too. Go and tell them to come around here if they got the sand. Me and Wyatt'll handle them, if they got the nerve to show their faces in Tombstone."

"Look," said Johnny Fletcher patiently, "we're on your side. We don't care for

Jim Fargo ourselves . . . "

"Good thing you don't, 'cause if there's one man I aim to kill me one of these days it's Jim Fargo . . . "

"You said it, Bill," Johnny agreed. "I've got no use for Jim Fargo. Or Jim Walker either, for that matter."

"Walker, bah! Him and his Silver Tombstone. My Little Boston's got more silver in a ton of ore than there is in Walker's whole mine."

A Buick convertible with the top down turned the corner a short distance away and skidded up in front of the house where Johnny and Sam were being abused by Bill Sage. A young, olive-skinned man of about thirty got out from behind the wheel and came toward the house. He showed fine white teeth in a huge grin.

"Hi, Bill!" he said cheerfully.

Bill Sage grinned back at the new arrival. "'Lo, Danny." He pointed a gnarled thumb at first Johnny, then Sam. "Couple of slickers tryin' to get my mine."

"Don't let 'em do it, Grandpa," said Danny. He winked at Johnny, then held out his hand. "My name's Danny Sage." As Johnny looked surprised, "Yep, I'm an Indian. Half, anyway. My mother was a full-blooded Hopi."

He chuckled suddenly. "Scared the hell out of you, didn't I?"

"Huh?"

"This morning." As Johnny still looked blank Danny Sage suddenly stooped forward, put one hand behind him and began a mock Indian dance. At the same time he patted one hand over his mouth and made a burlesqued Indian call.

Johnny gasped. "The snake-dancer!"

Sam Cragg cried out, "You're kidding."

"Not now," laughed Danny Sage. "But I was kidding this morning. You guys looked so funny when you popped up — guess you thought you'd stumbled in on some secret Indian ceremonies. As a matter of fact, I was trying to get some pictures for one of the picture magazines, to go along with an article I'm doing. Indian stuff." He shrugged. "The family was trying to help me out, by putting on one of the old time shows . . . "

Johnny was still dubious. "But you were the bird who had the rattlesnake in his mouth."

"Sure. Why not? The old boys used to do it. I can do anything they did . . . "

"Smart boy, Danny," said Old Man Sage. "Graduated from college before he was twenty."

Danny Sage winked again at Johnny. He seemed to like to wink. "What's this about a mine? You really interested in buying one?"

"Yes," said Johnny, "but not your grandfather's."

"There're a hundred mines around Tombstone; you can have almost any of them for about a dollar down. Of course if you want one with silver, that's another matter . . . "

"I'm interested in only one mine — the

Silver Tombstone . . . "

"That slag dump!" scoffed Old Bill.

"As a matter of fact," said Danny Sage, "The Silver Tombstone isn't in Tombstone; it's down south of Hansonville . . . "

"I know. I just stopped in to ask your grandfather about some of the old-timers around here . . . "

"Who?"

"Jim Walker . . . Jim Fargo . . . "

"Fargo's dead," suddenly exclaimed Bill Sage. "I remember the week before he died. Had a little run-in with him . . . "

"Sure, grandpa," said Danny Sage. "Look, I'll be over this evening to see you." He inclined his head toward his car. "I'll run you over to the Silver Tombstone . . . "

Johnny accepted the invitation promptly. "That's damn decent . . . "

"Not at all. Owe you something for that gag this morning . . . "

He started for the car. Johnny followed promptly, but Sam went reluctantly. Before he climbed in he examined the interior of the car with care and when Danny Sage raised an inquiring eyebrow, Sam scowled: "Snakes. Just lookin' to make sure there aren't any in the car."

Danny laughed. "I give you my word, pal."

The three of them got into the car, making a tight squeeze. Danny started the motor, shifted into high and made a quick U turn. He waved to his grandfather, then stepped on the gas pedal.

"Gramp's a great guy," he said, as the car roared away. "But he's eight-three and he gets mixed up."

"I found that out," replied Johnny. "What about that mine of his?"

Danny Sage made a wry face. "He hasn't had a mine since around 1899 — and it was shut down then for ten years. Most of the mines in Tombstone either played out in the late 'eighties or were flooded. Some of the old-timers have the theory that if the mines could be drained they'd be as rich as ever. But I don't know . . . "

The car was already through Tombstone and Danny made a sharp left turn onto an unpaved road. "What'd you want to know about Jim Fargo?" he asked suddenly.

"According to a piece I read in a book, the Silver Tombstone was discovered by his friend, Jim Walker, when he dug a grave to bury Fargo . . . "

"That's the story Walker told," Danny Sage said. "But it wasn't true."

"How do you know it wasn't?"

"I wrote a thesis on the old mines, for my master's degree," grinned Danny. "Did a lot of research for it — among my mother's people. They know things the white folks don't. They were around here. Nobody paid much attention to them, but they knew what was going on . . . Fargo knew about the silver all the time. He told Walker . . . and Walker bumped him off to get the mine."

"That isn't the way I read it in a

book called *Tombstone Days.*"

"No, it isn't. I read the book myself and might have swallowed that story, but ten years ago, when I wrote my thesis, my mother's uncle, Old Chief Vincento, was still alive. He told me the real story. He saw Walker do it."

"Saw him kill Fargo?" Johnny asked sharply.

Danny Sage nodded. "Yep!"

"Funny he didn't turn Walker in . . . "

"Why would he have done that?"

"Well, why wouldn't he?"

Danny looked sidewards at Johnny. "You don't know Indians, pal. Not the old-timers. They thought the white people were crazy scratching for gold and silver. And the whites . . . " he frowned a little. "Well, they thought the Indians were savages. An Indian wouldn't have been believed. Not in 1883 . . . "

He pointed ahead. "There's Hansonville."

15

DANNY SAGE had averaged a mile a minute Corning from Tombstone. He slackened his speed, however, to give Johnny and Sam the opportunity of seeing Hansonville. Only one quick glance was required, for Hansonville consisted of about a dozen tumbledown weathered shacks.

They continued through the little ghost town, picked up speed; then Danny slackened again as they neared a group of freshly-painted modern frame buildings, around which was a surprisingly new and strong steel fence, with a couple of strands of barbed wire on top. A sign over the top of one of the buildings read: HANSONVILLE MINING CORPORATION.

"The only real mine still around here," Danny commented. "Henderson's . . . "

Johnny stiffened. Since he was jammed

up against Danny Sage the latter could not help but feel the sudden hardening of Johnny's muscles. He looked sidewards. "Know Henderson?"

"You don't mean Mike Henderson, do you?" Sam Cragg blurted out.

"Why, yes. He was a classmate of mine at State U. Smart lad. His father left him a bankrupt cattle ranch and Mike right away goes out and finds himself a bonanza silver mine . . . Of course he took up metallurgy and mineralogy at the University, but so did I — and *I* haven't discovered any mines."

He suddenly braked the car, skidded it to a stop at the side of the little-used road. "Well, here we are," he exclaimed.

Johnny looked around the landscape. "Where?"

Danny Sage pointed. "Right there."

Johnny followed the pointing finger. He saw a weather-beaten shed some fifty yards from the road, a shed under which appeared to be a well.

"The Silver Tombstone," said Danny Sage.

He opened the door on his side and climbed out. Johnny followed, then Sam.

"Doesn't look like a mine to me," said Sam, voicing Johnny's own thoughts.

Danny Sage led the way toward the shed. "She doesn't look like much today, but she produced twelve million in her time. This hill," pointing to the sage-covered knoll behind the shed, "is the old slag dump. You can see that they brought out a lot of ore, at one time."

The slag dump was almost a hundred feet high and easily twice that many feet in area. The shed in front of it was merely a roof propped up on posts. In the center protruded a shaft containing a rusted, decrepit-looking winch and an elevator platform. The cable alone looked fairly new; it was well-greased.

"What's your interest in this hole?" Danny asked as Johnny examined the premises. "I know there's been a lot of talk about Tompkins striking a rich vein, but that's a lot of nonsense."

"What makes you think it is?"

"Because Tompkins hasn't done any more work on this mine than I have."

"Have *you* done any?"

Danny Sage shrugged. "I went down in it once or twice." He frowned and looked out over the landscape. Johnny followed his gaze and saw, almost a half a mile away, the buildings of the Hansonville Mining Corporation.

"Tell me," said Johnny, "is Henderson's mine paying out?"

"It was in bonanza a year ago and all reports have it that they've found a new vein," replied Danny Sage. "But I noticed the other day that they haven't got as many men working there as they used to have."

Johnny nodded thoughtfully. "Who's Joe Cotter?"

Danny Sage turned and looked Johnny in the eye. "What do you know about Joe Cotter?"

"I've met him."

Sam Cragg scowled. "If I meet him again, I'll murder him . . . "

"I'll make a bet on that," said Danny. "Joe's the strongest man in the state — maybe the entire Southwest."

"How much will you bet?" Johnny asked.

"You name it." Danny sized up Sam Cragg. After a moment he shook his head. "The build's all right — close to the ground, but I've got a cousin I think could throw you two falls out of three . . . "

"Bring him around," Sam challenged. "You saw him this morning."

"You can bring any two of *those* guys," Sam growled. "And Joe Cotter, too."

"Are you kidding?"

"My money's on Sam," said Johnny, "against any or all of your family — with Joe Cotter thrown in."

Danny Sage was again looking off. A twinkle came to his eyes. "You're lucky Joe Cotter's away."

There was a car coming up the road,

an open convertible. Johnny watched it as it came swiftly toward them. Then he exclaimed, "Joe Cotter!"

"Yeah," said Danny Sage. "Still want to make that bet?"

Sam Cragg promptly peeled off his coat. "This is the chance I've been waiting for."

"Wait a minute," said Johnny. "Helen Walker's with him."

"What of it?"

Joe Cotter pulled up his car behind that of Danny Sage. He jumped out from behind the wheel and ran around to help Helen Walker, but the latter was already out of the car.

The two came swiftly up the incline toward the Silver Tombstone. As they approached it became obvious that they had already recognized Johnny and Sam. Cotter strode ahead.

"I didn't think you could make it here," he exclaimed as he came up. "You're both under arrest."

"Ah-rr!" choked Sam, stepping forward.

Joe Cotter looked at him calmly. "The amateur strong man. Still want to tangle, eh?" He shook his head. "Sorry I can't oblige you. This is my bailiwick . . . "

Sam Cragg lunged for him, but Joe Cotter stepped swiftly aside and whipped out an automatic. "I represent the law around here," he snapped. "The California police are looking for you and I'm going to hold you for them . . . "

Sam Cragg faced Cotter. "Put down the roscoe," he dared. "Put it down and we'll see if you're as strong as you think you are."

"I'm strong enough to tie you into knots," said Joe Cotter.

Johnny Fletcher was looking steadily at Helen Walker. "That was a dirty trick," he said.

She averted her glance for a moment, then suddenly looked him squarely in the eye. "Yes — it was. I waited all evening. You could have telephoned, at least."

Joe Cotter reached out and grabbed Johnny roughly. The latter tried to shake him off, couldn't. He squirmed around. "Let go of me . . . "

Sam Cragg threw himself forward. Joe Cotter struck out at him with the automatic, but was handicapped through having hold of Johnny with his other hand. As a result he landed only a glancing blow on Sam's shoulder. Then Sam's thick arm swished down and cut across Cotter's forearm. The automatic flew out of Cotter's hand, sailed through the air and landed ten feet away. Danny Sage scooped it up.

"Now, you big slob," Sam Cragg snarled at Joe Cotter.

"Hold it!" snapped Danny Sage.

Sam Cragg caught hold of Joe Cotter's wrist, yanked heavily on it. Danny Sage pulled the trigger of the automatic and a bullet kicked up gravel near Sam's feet.

Sam let go of Joe Cotter and began to whirl. "I said — *hold it!*" Danny Sage repeated.

"Cutting yourself a piece of cake?" Johnny Fletcher asked, thinly.

"If there's any cake to cut — yes." He nodded toward Helen Walker. "I don't believe I've had the pleasure . . . "

Johnny said: "Miss Walker, Mr. Sage. He claims your great-uncle murdered Jim Fargo."

"I would say Mr. Sage is crazy," Helen Walker retorted promptly.

Danny Sage smiled pleasantly. "Mr. Fletcher didn't complete his statement. My mother's uncle — a full-blooded Hopi Indian — saw the job."

"I prefer to believe *my* great-uncle."

Danny Sage shrugged. "It doesn't really make any difference."

"No," said Johnny, "so how about putting up the gun?"

Joe Cotter said sharply: "All right, Danny — throw it over. I can handle this."

"You usually do, but I think it's time the Indian got back some of his. I'm in."

"You're in on what?" Cotter demanded.

227

"This," said Danny Sage, gesturing about him.

"I didn't think you'd be interested in the sand and gravel business."

"If *you're* interested in sand — I am."

"I'm the law here, that's all I'm interested in."

"What law?" asked Johnny Fletcher. "You're a lawyer, not a cop."

"Among other things I'm also a deputy sheriff."

Johnny looked at Danny Sage for confirmation. The latter nodded. "He's Mayor of Hansonville, deputy sheriff, jailer and also owns the grocery store."

Cotter bared his teeth. "Your number's up, wise guy. There's a murder rap waiting for you back in California."

"Murder?" Danny Sage's face showed sudden respect. "I didn't think you had it in you."

"I haven't. A little larceny maybe, but no murder. I never even met the victim until after he was dead." He looked thoughtfully at Danny Sage. "Didn't it make the papers out here?"

"I haven't been reading papers lately." Danny Sage nodded suddenly, coming to a decision. "Murder, eh? And you think it's only a matter of sand." He looked at the shaft, which led down into the vitals of the earth. "Maybe Dan Tompkins hit it, after all . . . The mine belongs to you, Miss Walker?"

"There's some difference of opinion about that," said Johnny. "Jim Walker has a grandson; a no-good from the looks of him. But anyway, Miss Walker had the mine willed to her and I imagine her claim to it is the best."

"Danny," said Joe Cotter ominously, "for the last time — hand over that gun and cut out the nonsense. You've got away with a lot of things in your time, but your family can't keep you out of trouble if you mix into this . . . "

"Take a walk, Joe," Danny Sage said.

"All right," Cotter said. He turned

to Helen Walker. "Coming?"

"I'll stay here," Helen said promptly.

"You, too?" Cotter's mouth twisted. "You might be making a mistake."

"I'll take the chance."

Without another word, Cotter strode off, heading for his car. The little group at the mine watched him go. Cotter reached his car, headed for the far side and leaning over opened the glove compartment. He took something out and ducked down behind his car.

A second later, a gun barked and lead kicked up sand near Danny Sage. Danny returned a quick snap shot, before springing for the meager shelter of the mine shaft. The others were not much behind him.

"He had another gun!" exclaimed Danny. He dropped to one knee, took careful aim and sent another bullet toward Cotter's car.

But Cotter's position was a more advantageous one, his car offering ideal shelter. The range was a little far for too accurate shooting but with time enough for careful aiming, Cotter — unless he was an atrociously bad shot — should score some hits.

He wasn't a bad shot as his next one proved. A bullet splintered wood about a half inch from Johnny's nose. He threw himself frantically onto the elevator platform. Then he was up on his feet instantly, stepping off and reaching for the fly wheel of the gasoline engine that operated the winch. He yanked viciously on the rope starter. The engine coughed, began roaring. A bullet from Cotter's gun clanged against the iron, ricocheted off into space.

"Get on the platform!" Johnny cried.

Danny Sage came over. "You get on — I'll let you down a few feet, out of range . . . "

Sam and Helen stepped onto the platform with alacrity. Johnny hesitated a moment, then stepped on the platform, stooping. Danny Sage sent two quick shots at Joe Cotter, then reached for the winch lever.

The descent into the shaft was so

swift that all three on the elevator were thrown off their feet. The platform went down into the dark shaft with frightening speed. Johnny clawed at the cable, got hold of it and braced himself. He turned up his face.

"Hey!" he yelled. "Not this far."

Helen Walker cried out in sudden fear. But the elevator continued to plummet down into the earth. The opening above grew smaller and smaller. And after a moment or two it became a mere pinpoint of light.

Then the elevator stopped so suddenly that they were again thrown into a heap.

"Godalmighty!" choked Sam Cragg, picking himself up. "He let us drop all the way down."

"Maybe he was hit," said Johnny and a sudden shudder ran through him.

The blackness in the shaft was Stygian. Johnny picked himself up and reached out with a hand. It touched slimy earth. He groped about, brushed clothing that he assumed was Helen

Walker's. She was sobbing.

He reached into his pocket and found a book of paper matches. He struck one, held it for a moment until it burned bright. Then he took a step forward, off the elevator platform onto solid shale.

"There's a shaft here," he announced.

The match burned his finger and he dropped it. Fumbling, he struck another and noted that there were only about a half dozen in the book. He took a couple of steps into the shaft and exclaimed.

On a wooden shelf stood a half dozen carbide lamps. He picked up one, shook it and heard water slosh inside. He touched the match end to the opening, but no gas light shot into flame. He realized then that the lamp was empty of carbide. The match in his hand was burning short, too.

Just as it went out he saw a round tin canister on another shelf, stepped forward and struck a third match. As he had guessed the canister contained carbide. He heaved a sigh of relief, opened the canister and lamp and dumped carbide from the canister into the lamp. He sloshed water on it and applied a fourth match to the opening. A bright white flame shot out.

He turned and found Sam and Helen behind him. He handed Helen the lamp, fixed two more, one for himself and one for Sam.

"How do we get out, climb up the cable?" Sam asked.

Johnny stepped back to the elevator shaft, stooped and peered down under the platform. He got to his feet again and shook his head, soberly.

"This is the bottom."

"All right," growled Sam. "I haven't done any rope climbing for quite awhile, but if I have to, I guess I can climb fifty feet, hand over hand."

"Can you climb six hundred feet?" Johnny asked.

"Six hundred! We didn't fall that far . . ."

"I'm afraid we did. This is the bottom of the shaft, the six hundred foot level . . ."

"How do you know it's six hundred feet?"

"The book — *Tombstone Days* . . ."

Helen Walker nodded. "That's right. But isn't it possible that part of the shaft caved in and that we didn't come down all the way?"

"Take a look up," Johnny suggested. "That opening is six feet square . . . it looks like a pin point. All right, say it's the five hundred foot level."

"That doesn't make it any easier," said Helen. "What do you . . . suppose has happened up above?"

Johnny shrugged, expressively. "Your guess is as good as mine . . ."

"That damned Indian!" Sam swore suddenly. "He's as bad as Cotter. Chewing that rattlesnake this morning should've warned me . . ."

Helen Walker gave Sam Cragg an odd look and took a step closer to Johnny. Despite the seriousness of the situation, Johnny couldn't help chuckling.

"He hasn't blown his top," he assured Helen. "We were . . . uh . . . taking a shortcut across the desert this morning and came across an Indian village. They were having a snake dance — and Danny Sage was one of the dancers. He had a rattlesnake in his mouth."

Helen shuddered.

"He was only trying to get some pictures for *Life* or *Look*," Johnny said.

"That's what *he* said," Sam growled. "I been thinking. That was pretty neat the way he got us away from Old Bill Sage . . . and why'd he bring us all the way out here?"

"That's an interesting question, Sam." Johnny rubbed his chin with the back of his free hand. "Danny's grandfather knew your great-uncle, Helen. And Old Bill Sage."

"Rooster Bill!" exclaimed Helen. "I've heard Uncle Jim talk about him."

"Rooster Bill?"

"Because he was always crowing."

"He's still crowing," laughed Johnny. "According to him, Wyatt Earp, Curly Bill and Jim Fargo were a bunch of punks. He used to slap them around something. . . "

He broke off and suddenly sprang forward. But he was too late. The elevator platform, which had suddenly creaked, sprang up into the shaft. Johnny's clutching fingers barely scraped the edge of it.

"He's pulled it up!"

"Who?" cried Helen.

"We'll know in a few minutes," said Johnny.

"How?" asked Sam. "If he comes down he can't operate the thing, can he?"

"No," frowned Johnny. "The starter's up above." He muttered under his breath. "We should have stayed on the platform. Well — maybe not. Joe Cotter may have won upstairs. That wouldn't be good for us."

"If Danny won he'll send the elevator

down again for us, won't he?" Helen's voice was pregnant with hope.

"Oh, sure," Johnny said, although he was not nearly as hopeful as was Helen. He turned and looked gloomily down the tunnel leading away from the elevator shaft. The light from the three carbide lamps showed glistening walls, but did not penetrate the tunnel for more than a few feet.

"Call me if the elevator starts down," Johnny said.

Sam exclaimed, "Where are you going, Johnny?"

"I want to see what's down here. I won't go far . . . "

"I'll go with you," Helen volunteered.

"Better wait here."

"No, I'd rather go with you."

"I don't like this place any more than anyone else," growled Sam Cragg.

"All right," said Johnny, "we'll all go exploring. And if the elevator comes down . . . "

"It'll wait for us," said Helen.

"We hope."

16

WITH the others following, Johnny struck out down the tunnel. It was straight and level for about fifty feet, then made a sharp right turn and dropped at least twenty feet during the next thirty yards. Then it made another turn.

There were tunnels running off at angles every few yards from the main one, but they were smaller and so obviously lesser ones that Johnny had no difficulty in deciding which was the main one and he kept to it.

But after traveling about five minutes they came to a cave-in which blocked the main tunnel. They turned back then to the first side tunnel and saw that it had been used more or less recently.

Johnny stopped. "Maybe we'd better get back to the elevator," he suggested.

"I been thinkin' that ever since we started." Sam agreed, quickly.

Helen Walker shook her head. "Let's see where this one leads to."

Johnny hesitated a moment, then turned into the secondary tunnel. It was a winding one and not too well shored up, for every few yards there were heaps of dirt and shale, which had caved in from the ceiling or walls. But they continued on.

Behind Johnny, Sam Cragg suddenly cried out in alarm. Johnny whirled. "Cut it out, Sam!" he exclaimed testily.

"My lamp," Sam retorted, holding it out toward Johnny. "It's gone out."

Johnny winced. He hadn't noticed that at first. But now he took Sam's lamp and shook it. There was only a tiny rattle inside. Quickly he opened the lamp and shook a small lump of carbide into his palm.

Helen Walker inhaled softly. Her own lamp was sputtering and the flame was becoming smaller. Johnny leaned over quickly and blew it out.

"I think we better start back," he announced grimly.

"Yes," said Helen, quietly. "I don't think it would be fun wandering around here in the dark."

Darkness came sooner than Johnny thought, for they had gone less than fifty feet in a backward direction when his own lamp became feeble. He blew it out and in darkness took the small lump of carbide from Sam's lamp, added to it what remained in Helen's and put it all in his own lamp. Then he relit the thing. The flame burned brighter. For about two minutes. Then it went out — completely.

"This is it," Johnny said.

"We ought to be within a few yards of the main tunnel," Helen said, in the darkness. "Once we hit that we shouldn't have any trouble."

"*If* we hit it," said Johnny. "There are about a million small tunnels here. We'll have to stop at every cross-tunnel and feel if it's the right size . . . And I guess we'd better keep close together."

For reply Helen groped for Johnny and found his hand. Then she reached with her other hand for Sam Cragg. Hand in hand, they started again, Helen in the center and Johnny and Sam on each side, and with their free hands groping for the walls. After a moment or two Sam announced a tunnel and they paused to size it up, by feel. The decision as to whether it was a small tunnel or the larger main one, was surprisingly difficult to make, for in the dark size was hard to determine.

But they finally agreed that it was a smaller tunnel and continued on. The next tunnel was a long time in coming. It seemed larger than the previous one and they turned into it. Then came an even larger tunnel — or so it seemed.

Johnny gritted his teeth. "This isn't right," he said. "The first tunnel was the one we should have turned into."

"But it was smaller than this one," Helen protested.

"Was it? Or did it just seem so? I

think we traveled too far before we turned into the last one. If we make one more mistake we're done for. I think the best thing is to turn back now, while we can still hope to find the last tunnel."

"But are you sure you can?"

Johnny hesitated. "No," he said, finally. "As far as I'm concerned, we're lost now."

Helen pulled her hand from Johnny's grip. "Why I ever threw in with you, I don't know."

"I was wondering about that myself."

"Hey!" cried Sam. "Let's not start fighting *now*."

"I'm not fighting," Helen retorted.

Johnny bared his teeth in the darkness. "I'm not either, but there are still some questions I'm going to ask you . . . when we're where I can see your face."

"You've still got some matches, haven't you?" Helen challenged.

Johnny reached into his pocket, felt for the paper book. He found it and brought it out of his pocket. His fingers told him, however, that there was one bone match in it. He folded the book and returned it to his pocket. There might be a more urgent need for a match later.

"No," he said, "I used the last one when I relit the lamp."

"You fool!" cried Helen Walker in sudden anger. Johnny accepted the designation. "I guess you're right."

"Now, wait a minute, Johnny," said Sam Cragg, alarm in his voice. "If we ever get out of here its you that'll have to find the way, Johnny — not me. Don't go giving up."

"I'm not," said Johnny. "Not yet."

Suddenly he reached out in the darkness. "Helen?" he asked, sharply. "Where are you?"

"Here," replied her voice — from some distance away.

He started in the direction he thought her voice came from. But he stopped after a few feet. "Where?" he called.

"Over here," her voice replied — and

244

seemed farther away than ever.

Muttering, he turned back swiftly, and collided with Sam Cragg.

"This is me," Sam exclaimed.

"Hang onto me," Johnny ordered. "Helen!" he called again.

For a moment there was no reply at all. Then her voice called, fainter than before: "Yes!"

"Don't move!" Johnny cried. "Stay where you are and I'll find you."

"All right," was her reply.

Sam was clutching Johnny's arm and together they moved a few feet. "Answer now," Johnny said.

"I'm here," came her voice.

A cold sweat broke out over Johnny's body. He was sure now that she was in an altogether different direction than the one in which he had been moving.

"Hold on," he advised Sam in a whisper. Then he moved carefully one step, two, and reaching out, touched a wall. He made a careful about face, paced off three steps and touched the opposite wall. Then he made a right face and with Sam holding onto his arm, went a dozen counted steps.

"Now where are you?" he called.

"Johnny!" Helen's voice came faintly and hysterically. "You're farther away than ever."

Johnny swore softly. "All right," he cried, "*I'll* stand still and *you* come toward me. I've gotten mixed up, somehow . . . "

There was silence for a long moment. Then Johnny could stand it no longer. "Are you coming?"

There was no reply!

"Helen!" Johnny roared at the top of his voice. "Where are you?"

"Here!" came a faint, a very faint reply.

In sudden panic, Johnny sprang forward and collided with the tunnel wall so hard that his head spun for a moment. When it cleared, he tried yelling again.

Sam took it up, bellowing at the top of his voice. The sound echoed and re-echoed through the tunnels, but there was no reply.

Helen Walker was lost.

So were they, for that matter, but there is something less terrifying if two people are together when lost.

Johnny and Sam made desperate attempts to find her. They paced off distances, returned and went in the opposite direction. They found side tunnels, venturing into them. They called and they listened. Once or twice they thought they heard faint cries and immediately went in the direction from which they believed the sound came. But it was never repeated — at least not from the same direction.

Time went by. Neither Johnny nor Sam had watches, but Johnny guessed that two or three hours had elapsed since they had entered the tunnel. It would be evening up on top of the earth.

"Let's face it, Sam," Johnny said. "Shall we sit down and wait for it, or shall we keep moving . . . until we drop?"

"How big can a mine like this be?" Sam exclaimed.

"I don't know. I know very little about mines. Sure, I've read about them, but never had any particular reason to remember the details. I seem to have some recollection, though, of reading that these old-time mines sometimes had miles of tunnels . . . "

"But they've got to end somewhere, don't they?" Sam cried. "Don't mines have limits?"

"Not especially. The old rule is that a mine can follow a vein, no matter where it leads — as long as it begins on its own property." He scowled in the inky blackness. "It's the damn cross-tunnels that get me."

"How many of those can there be?"

"Hundreds."

"You're sure of that?"

"I'm not sure of anything," said Johnny. "Let me think; it seems I read once that claims were only a hundred feet wide. Yet, I remember somewhere else something about fifteen

248

hundred feet . . . Must be different rules for different states. Wait a minute . . . When we were up top, how far did it seem to Henderson's place?"

"About a half mile."

"All right, say a half mile, then — that's saying this mine runs all the way to the edge of the Henderson one; we're not sure of that, but let's count it the worst way and say that it does. That's roughly two thousand five hundred feet . . . and these crosscut tunnels seem to pop up every sixty or seventy feet; let's give ourselves the worst of it and say fifty feet; that should be two every hundred feet . . . fifty tunnels at the outside, not counting the ten feet or so that each tunnel occupies. So there couldn't possibly be more than fifty crosscut tunnels, probably only thirty-five or forty. And let's say each one runs a half mile — which I doubt. Fifty times a half mile, that would be twenty-five miles. Shall we try them — one after the other, to the end, then back . . . "

Johnny swore. "I forgot the back-trail each time. That doubles everything. All right, fifty miles."

"Fifty miles in the dark," Sam said, bitterly. "Let's get moving . . . But what are we looking for?"

"Helen Walker," Johnny said.

"And after we find her?"

"The elevator."

"And what if it's up?"

"Let's talk about that when we find it . . . At least we'll have light then; there was plenty of carbide in that can."

"It's no good without a match to light it."

"I've got a match — one match. I was saving it for emergencies."

They started out in the darkness, arms locked together, their free hands stretched out to touch walls, against which they bumped repeatedly, for in the blackness their feet could not travel in straight lines, even if the tunnels did sometimes run fairly straight.

They stumbled along in silence for some minutes, when they encountered a cross-shaft. Johnny called a halt and he grimly measured the distance across the tunnel in which they had been traveling. He did it by getting down on the floor and measuring with his arms, then with a sliver from one of the shoring beams that he pried loose.

He came to the conclusion that the tunnel in which they had been traveling was about six feet wide, or roughly three lengths of the piece of wood. He crawled carefully then to the new tunnel and measured it.

"Eight feet!" he announced exultantly. "It must be the main tunnel."

"Let's go!" cried Sam Cragg.

They went blithely down the new tunnel, but had proceeded less than fifty feet when they came abruptly to a cave-in — either a cave-in, or the end of the digging. They tested it to the ceiling, found it solid, then hopefully turned and began retracing their steps, figuring that the new direction would bring them back to the elevators. A hundred feet brought them up against a solid wall.

"What the hell!" cried Johnny.

Sam Cragg groaned.

"We're cooked."

Sam was silent for a moment. "What do you suppose the Indian would do . . . if he won the fight upstairs and knew we were down here?"

"I *hope* he'd come down and search for us."

"You don't really think he would, though?"

"I don't know," Johnny said, frankly. "There're some funny things about Danny Sage. I've been thinking about him and I don't think I'd trust him very far."

"That was damn funny the way he let us down all the way into the mine," Sam speculated. "He said he'd drop us just a few feet — out of the range of the bullets."

"That's one of the things that keeps sticking in my mind. All right, suppose Joe Cotter won. He doesn't like us, but he's a cop. It's his duty to try to arrest us. But does he really want to arrest us? He's in this Silver Tombstone business up to his neck . . . Remember what Tompkins said."

Sam exclaimed. "Say, there's the bird knows his way around this mine. Didn't he say he'd explored down here for two years?"

"Yes. He ought to know these shafts and tunnels pretty well. But he's over in California."

"Maybe not — Joe Cotter and the girl were there, and they're here today."

"That's one of the questions I was going to ask her — how she happened to show up here with Joe Cotter. They were supposed to be on opposite sides. There was something about her I didn't tell you, Sam, something that happened in the hotel in Hollywood . . . while you were following Charles Ralston down to the morgue . . . She came to see me: And she left a few minutes before the cops broke in."

"She squealed on you?"

"That's what I thought at the time. It made me sore . . . because she hadn't acted like that while she was in the room with me."

"What do you mean — like *that*?"

Johnny cleared his throat. "As a matter of fact, she was, ah, *quite* friendly."

"*How* friendly?"

"I kissed her."

"Yeah?" The tone was an invitation for additional revelations. Despite the seriousness of the moment Johnny couldn't help chuckling. "That's all. I made more or less of a date for that evening with her, but after the cops showed up I figured she'd put the finger on me. Maybe she did. I don't know. But if we ever . . . " His voice broke off. Then suddenly he inhaled sharply. "Sam!" he cried softly. "Did you see something . . . a light?"

Sam was startled. "A light?"

"Give me a lift."

Quickly Sam caught Johnny about the waist and raised him toward the ceiling. Johnny cracked his head on the roof, then stiffened in Sam's grasp.

"There *is* a light, Sam," he said. "Pretty far off, but it's moving. Let me down . . . "

Sam lowered Johnny quickly to the floor and the latter leaped forward. He hit the cave-in, but in view of what he had seen, began groping upwards quickly. He exclaimed again. "This cave-in isn't all the way to the ceiling, Sam. The light's beyond it — the tunnel continues. Let's see if we can't get over this . . . "

Sam was already at his side, his fingers tearing away at the earth. They worked at terrific speed for a moment or two, digging like gophers. Then they had a space large enough at the top for even Sam to crawl through.

A moment later they were in the tunnel on the other side of the cave-in. But the light had gone.

"I don't care," Johnny said, doggedly. "I saw it — straight ahead, three or four hundred feet."

"Maybe we should've yelled."

"I thought of that."

"Then why didn't you?"

"I thought we'd better play it this way. Come on . . . "

They proceeded swiftly down the tunnel, arms again locked, hands stretched out to ward themselves off the tunnel walls. They traveled a hundred paces, two hundred, then hit a solid wall. But a tunnel cut off at right angles and at the end of it — was a streak of yellow light.

Sam and Johnny broke into a run. As they neared the yellow light it became brighter and suddenly bursting around a turn in the tunnel they saw ahead of them — suspended from the ceiling — a lighted electric bulb!

"We're saved!" Sam babbled.

"Maybe," said Johnny. "But this isn't the Silver Tombstone — they didn't have electric power there."

"I don't care what it is, but let's get out of here . . . Help!" The last word was yelled at the top of his lungs. The

256

response was immediate.

"Who's there?" cried a voice.

"Here!" replied Johnny.

A man popped out of a cubicle, stared at Johnny and Sam.

"What the hell!"

"Where are we?" Johnny asked.

"Don't you know?"

"We got lost in the Silver Tombstone . . ."

"The Silver Tombstone!" cried the other man. "This is the Hansonville mine . . . how could you get lost in the Silver Tombstone and show up here?"

"That I don't know. But we've been wandering around in the Silver Tombstone for hours . . ." Johnny cleared his throat. "What time is it?"

The man pulled out a big nickeled watch. "'Bout four."

"In the afternoon?"

"Morning. Don't you — *know*?"

"I didn't have the slightest idea. That means we were wandering around more than twelve hours." Johnny turned, looked over his shoulder. "Isn't there a shift working here?"

"Not any more. We on'y got a day shift going now. I'm sort of a watchman . . . although I don't know what there is to watch. Boss's orders, though."

"Who came by a few minutes ago?"

"Are you kidding?"

"No. We saw a light a few minutes ago. A moving light. That's how we happened to come here."

The face of the watchman showed worry. "Ain't no one down here this time of night except myself." He hesitated. "And you fellows." Then he added, "I hope."

"There was a woman with us in the Silver Tombstone," Johnny said. "We lost her in the darkness."

The watchman suddenly backed away. "Look, fellows, I'm only the watchman here. I don't know anything . . . about anything."

Johnny nodded. "How do we get out of here?"

"The elevator," said the watchman.

"This way . . . " He walked swiftly ahead of Johnny and Sam, made a sharp right turn and brought up against a wire cage. He pressed a button.

"It'll be down in a minute."

"What about upstairs? Anyone on watch there?"

The watchman hesitated, then added, "Old Byron."

The elevator shaft was already whining and a moment later a closed elevator slid to a stop before the grilled door. The door opened automatically. Johnny and Sam stepped into the elevator, waved to the watchman.

Johnny reached for a button inside the elevator, but before his finger touched it, the door closed and the elevator began moving upwards.

"Something screwy in this place," Sam Cragg muttered.

"The words out of my mouth," said Johnny.

"The ghost down there — it couldn't have been Helen Walker?"

Johnny's forehead wrinkled. "If so,

Question One: where'd she get a light? Number Two: why go flitting around the tunnels when she could come forward like us?"

The elevator began slowing up and suddenly came to an abrupt halt. A grilled door rose and Johnny and Sam stepped out of the elevator, to face a grizzled, astonished man who was holding a very capable-looking sawed-off shotgun.

"What the . . . ?" he began.

"What the hell!" Johnny shot out. "My name's Fletcher; this is Sam Cragg. And how are *you* . . . ?"

The shotgun pointed at Johnny's stomach. "Where'd you come from?" Old Byron demanded.

"Downstairs. The six hundred foot level. We broke through from the Silver Tombstone . . . "

Old Byron's eyes widened even more. "Ain't no one working the Silver Tombstone . . . "

"We were prospecting it."

"Yeah, but she don't touch our

mine." The old watchman shook his head doggedly. "Gotta report this to the boss."

"Mike Henderson? He's in California."

"Who says so?"

"You mean he's back?"

"Talked to him less'n an hour ago."

"Here?"

"What's wrong about that? He lives here, don't he?"

Johnny nodded. "All right, rouse him out."

"Oh, he ain't gone to bed yet." Byron gestured with his head, then stepped aside smartly so neither Johnny nor Sam would be able to reach the shotgun.

Johnny and Sam exchanged glances, then started for a door that was apparently indicated. Johnny opened it and stepped out into the open air. He drew a deep breath. Awhile back he had given up hope of ever breathing fresh air again.

"Straight ahead," ordered the watchman.

17

JOHNNY started down a flagged walk, turned a corner around a darkened building and saw straight ahead a neat-looking cottage, with lighted windows.

"Oh, Mr. Henderson!" the watchman called.

The door of the cottage opened, framing Mike Henderson, fully dressed, in the lighted doorway.

"What is it?" he called testily.

"Here's a couple of fellas just come up from the mine. Claim they broke through from the Silver Tombstone . . ."

Johnny stepped into the light from the doorway and Mike Henderson suddenly recognized him.

"I'll be a monkey's uncle!"

"Me, too," said Johnny.

"Byron," said Mike Henderson, "stay out here."

"Shore will, Mr. Henderson." The old watchman patted the stock of the shotgun. "Yell if you want me."

Henderson stepped out of the doorway. "Come in, boys. I think we ought to have a little talk — about things."

"Why not? It's only four-five A.M."

Henderson chuckled. "They never get you down, do they?"

"I've been down," Johnny said sagely. "But now that I'm up, nothing will ever get me down again." He winked at Sam Cragg, who was more cheerful than he had been in days. They had come through a trying ordeal — and Johnny Fletcher was his old, chipper self. That was good enough for Sam.

Johnny and Sam walked into Mike Henderson's cottage and Henderson followed and closed the door. Inside the living room he went to a table at which he had evidently been working and threw a newspaper over some papers and drawings.

"All right," he said then. "Let's have the story."

"You won't believe it," said Johnny.

"I won't believe what? Joe Cotter and Danny Sage were here last night. I didn't believe *them*, but I'm willing to believe *you* . . . now."

"What'd they tell you?"

"Let's have your story first."

Johnny crossed to a big Morris chair, dropped in it and stretched out his legs. "You tell *me*."

"Now wait a minute," said Henderson. "You came out of my mine — trespassing . . . "

"Well," said Johnny, "you may have something there. Okay, I'll tell you, the story. Joe Cotter and Danny Sage made a deal."

"What do you mean — a deal?"

"Why, the last time I saw both of them they were exchanging bullets . . . "

"When was that?"

"Around four yesterday afternoon."

"They were shooting at each other? Where . . . ?"

"Over at the Silver Tombstone. To make a long story short, Danny Sage

264

drove Sam and me out to the mine. We'd hardly got there when Joe Cotter showed up . . . "

"Alone?"

Johnny hesitated. "No, he had someone with him."

Henderson nodded in satisfaction. "All right, I was just wondering if you were going to tell me a story . . . As a matter of fact, Joe Cotter stopped here and picked up Helen."

"But he didn't bring her back."

Mike Henderson picked up a celluloid draftsman's rule and began toying with it. "What happened at the Silver Tombstone?"

"Nothing special. Joe Cotter and Danny began shooting at each other, that's all. And Danny wanted to protect us, so he let us down into the mine. And forgot to pull us up again."

"You and — " Henderson nodded toward Sam Cragg.

"And Helen Walker."

"Helen Walker went down into the mine with you?"

"She's there yet."

"No, I'm not," said the voice of Helen Walker.

Johnny Fletcher sprang to his feet and faced Helen Walker, coming out of a bedroom.

"Holy Mother!" breathed Sam Cragg.

Johnny stared at her. It was Helen Walker, all right; Helen Walker wearing pajamas and dressing gown and as fresh as though she'd just enjoyed a good night's sleep.

Johnny seated himself and weariness flowed into his body.

"I quit," he said.

Sam Cragg was breathing hoarsely and his eyes threatened to pop from his head. Then he suddenly began growling and moved uneasily toward the door.

Mike Henderson came toward Johnny Fletcher and stood over him, his feet wide apart.

"Now let's have the real story."

"You tell me," Johnny said heavily. "You and . . . " he inclined his head toward her, " . . . Helen."

"*My* story's simple enough," said Helen Walker. "I just walked over to the elevator shaft and rode up to the surface."

Johnny groaned, "Oh, Stop it!"

"That's the truth."

" . . . The elevator just happened to be there . . . and it just happened to go up when you stepped into it?"

"Not exactly. Danny Sage was on the elevator and Joe Cotter operated the winch."

"I'll believe that part," Johnny said. "Danny and Joe got together. But you said you *just* walked over to the elevator shaft . . . *Just* like that!"

"It wasn't hard, once I got my bearings. The map is quite accurate."

Johnny sat up. "What map?"

"The map of the mine — the shafts and all that."

"You had that map all the time?"

"In my purse. Along with a pencil flashlight."

"Goddamit!" cried Sam Cragg.

"Goddamit to hell."

Johnny held up a chiding finger. "There's a lady present, Sam . . . I think." He turned back to Helen. "Of course you didn't know you had the map — and the flashlight, when you were still with us . . . "

"Oh, I knew all the time that I had them." Helen smiled pleasantly. "As a matter of fact, I didn't *stray* away from you. I left you, deliberately."

Johnny got up from the chair. Mike Henderson stepped forward and held out a hand.

"Sam!" Johnny said sharply.

Sam advanced upon Henderson. The latter backed away. "Byron!" he yelled at the top of his voice.

Heels clicked upon the macadam outside. "I'm comin'," cried the voice of Old Byron, the watchman.

The door slammed open. By that time Sam Cragg was beside it. Byron charged in and Sam reached out and took the shotgun from him as easily as if it had been a toy and Byron a

268

child. The old watchman cried out in chagrin.

Laura Henderson appeared from the bedroom. She too, was in negligee and wearing a dressing gown. "Do we have to have these scenes in the middle of the night?" she asked.

"This one's over now," Johnny replied. "You can go back to bed."

"It isn't over yet, Fletcher," Mike Henderson said, darkly. "Maybe I can't prevent your walking out of here, but where're you going to go? The desert isn't big enough to hide you and in the morning Joe Cotter will be on your trail. Joe Cotter and some of Danny Sage's relatives. They can trail a tarantula across the desert. You're a murderer and . . . "

"I'm not a murderer," Johnny exclaimed impatiently. "How many times do I have to tell people that?"

"You didn't do a good job of convincing the California police. In fact, your running away was proof . . . "

"Stop it, Mike," cut in Laura

Henderson. "You're wearing out that record . . . "

"I'll play it until the cows come home. Fletcher and this gorilla were at that motel in San Bernardino. Hugh Kitchen was found in their car — and they've been trying to cut in on the Silver Tombstone ever since. What more do you want?"

"A lot more than that," Johnny said. "Sam and I stopped at the motel by sheer accident. We'd never even heard of Hugh Kitchen. We'd never heard of the Silver Tombstone . . . "

"But you've heard plenty about it since then. And you threw in with Tompkins, the damned crook." Mike Henderson shook his head angrily. "Pokes around in the Silver Tombstone for two years, then pretends he's found a rich vein . . . Yes, he found it all right . . . in *my* mine."

"In your mine?"

"What do you suppose this is all about? You can buy all the silver in the Silver Tombstone for a silver dollar.

270

Tompkins wants to own the mine so he can dig into *my* mine . . . "

"That isn't true, Mike," Helen Walker said suddenly. "I thought we'd agreed . . . "

"I agreed to pay you fifty thousand for the Silver Tombstone," Henderson stated. "I didn't agree that there was a rich vein in your mine."

"Then why would you pay fifty thousand dollars for it?"

"Because the lawsuits would cost more. I know all about the apex laws and I don't want to get involved in them. Some stupid judge might even decide against me; so I'm willing to pay fifty thousand dollars . . . "

"To buy me off?"

"If you want to put it that way — yes."

"Well, I don't want to put it that way. The deal is off . . . "

"Now wait a minute!" cried Henderson. "You agreed . . . "

"I agreed, but I didn't sign. I'm not taking charity."

271

"Attagirl!" said Laura Henderson.

"Keep out of this, Laura," Henderson snarled. "There're some things you don't know."

"Not very many."

"What's an apex law?" Johnny asked.

Henderson gestured impatiently. "This isn't the time for a course in mining law."

"An apex law," Laura Henderson began to explain, in defiance of her brother, "means that a mine owner can follow a vein wherever it leads, into adjoining mines even, provided only that the vein apexes — or begins — on his own claim. And it is virtually impossible to prove where a vein apexes . . . "

"Then what's the sense of the law?" Johnny asked.

"Lawyers have to live, don't they? It's a vicious law, in the hands of unscrupulous miners and lawyers. Up in Deadwood, South Dakota, George Hearst had to spend twenty-six million dollars in buying up adjoining claims just to protect his Homestake Mine from apex suits. And the Anaconda Copper Corporation paid F. Augustus Heinze eleven million for a claim consisting of nineteen square feet. They didn't pay the money for the nineteen square feet, but to settle some one hundred and fifty suits that Heinze had outstanding against them at the time. Or that they had against Heinze . . . "

"Laura," Mike Henderson broke in impatiently, "what's the sense of all that?"

"I think Johnny Fletcher should have all the information he needs," retorted Laura Henderson, "for if anyone is going to settle this mess, he's the one."

"Why, thanks," said Johnny, surprised.

"He can settle it," said Mike Henderson angrily, "by confessing."

"You're a stubborn cuss," Johnny said. "Once you get your mind made up about something nothing can change it."

"Nothing but proof otherwise."

"Lend me a hundred dollars," said Johnny, "and I'll get you the proof."

"I'd just as soon burn a hundred dollars as give it to you."

Laura Henderson went into her bedroom. She returned in a moment with two fifty dollar bills. "Here's the money!" She handed the bills to Johnny.

"Laura!" cried Mike Henderson.

"It's my money."

"You're a fool."

"Maybe I am," Laura said calmly. "And maybe *you're* the one who's the fool. All I know is that Fletcher arrived in California without a cent and within a short time was flashing fifty dollar bills — "

"Stolen, no doubt!" cut in Mike Henderson.

"Perhaps. But at any rate he had enough ingenuity to get the money. Then he was arrested, escaped, and with the police of the entire state after him, he was able to go clear across the state, and almost through another. He's had a lot of people working against him and he's come through. I say he's got something. And I'm willing to string along with him."

"You'll regret it."

"No, she won't," Johnny said. "She's the second smartest person in this setup. I say second, because the smartest one is the one who murdered Hugh Kitchen — the one I'm going to nail for you with this hundred dollars."

"You understand," said Mike Henderson, "you're taking that money at the point of a gun — "

"He isn't!" cried Laura. "I gave him the money."

"You haven't any money of your own. Whatever you have you've gotten from me."

"Mike," said Johnny, "you're becoming an awfully obnoxious guy."

"All this talk isn't going to get us anywhere, Johnny," interrupted Sam. "It'll be morning in a little while and we want to be on our way by then."

"A long ways, too," said Johnny. He looked around the circle of faces. "Goodbye, now."

Laura Henderson was the only one who replied. "Goodbye, Johnny Fletcher . . . and good luck."

Johnny opened the door and stepped out. Sam followed, making a threatening gesture with the shotgun before closing the door.

18

THE grey dawn was already breaking, Johnny noted. He shook his head. Mike Henderson was probably already at the telephone. Within ten minutes, Joe Cotter would be out. There wasn't enough time.

Or was there.

A station wagon stood inside an open garage. Johnny glanced quickly at Sam and headed for the vehicle. The keys were in it, which would save them the couple of minutes it would have taken them to fashion a wire spark-jumper.

"You'll notice," said Sam, as he climbed into the station wagon beside Johnny, "I ain't even afraid of stealing a car any more."

"We're only borrowing this for a little while."

The starter caught instantly and Johnny backed the station wagon out of the garage, turned it on the macadam and headed for a wire gate fifty feet away.

He stopped in front of the gate and Sam sprang out and opened it. They didn't bother to close it. Johnny turned the car left, in the direction of Hansonville. Sam grunted.

"All right, I hope we run into him."

"Joe?"

"Who else?"

They sped through the little hamlet and negotiated the graveled road to Tombstone probably faster than it had ever been covered before.

At Tombstone they turned left once more on the main paved road. The speedometer indicated sixty-five a minute after they left the town and Johnny pressed his foot down upon the accelerator. The needle shot up to seventy, advanced to seventy-five, then eighty. It hovered there for a little while, then Johnny began easing off. When the needle got down to sixty, Sam looked at him puzzled.

"Ought to be hitting it any minute," Johnny said.

"Hitting what?"

"The filling station where we left our car . . . "

"What do you want to go back there for?" Sam ejaculated.

"To pick up our car — naturally. That's why I borrowed the money from Laura Henderson . . . Ha!"

He began braking and then swung the car to the left, off the road into the filling station. It was dark, but there were two cars parked at the side of the station; one a battered jalopy, the other the Chevrolet that Johnny and Sam had deserted so precipitately the night before.

Johnny kept the motor running, but blasted the night with the horn. Sam patted the stock of the shotgun.

A light appeared in the living quarters behind the station. Johnny pressed down two or three times more on the horn, then shut off the motor.

"Okay, Sam," he said, "but keep the

gun behind you for a minute."

A light went on in the filling station, revealing the old proprietor. He was wearing a long nightshirt and gesturing angrily.

"Go 'way," he shouted.

Johnny stepped up to the glass door so the man inside could recognize him. He put his hand up to the glass, to show the money in it.

"Open up," he yelled back. "I want to pay you the money I owe you."

The old man's assistant appeared, clad also in a nightshirt, but carrying the old man's long revolver. Luke Johnson came to the door and unlocked it.

"What're you trying to pull?" he demanded.

"I want my car," Johnny said. "I owe you one twenty-eight; here's your money."

"Well, I'll be a Gila monster!" sputtered the old man. He took the money from Johnny's hand, began counting it.

"I hope you ground the valves," Johnny said pointedly, "because I've paid for the job and if you haven't done the work I'll report you to the Automobile Club."

"I ground them yesterday," said Lafe, "but I discovered that your generator was shot. I put a new one in; cost you twenty-eight fifty . . ."

Sam brought the shotgun out from behind his back. "How much?"

Lafe took one look and dropped the revolver. Johnny scooped it up. "Now give me the key to my car."

The two filling station men backed into the station. "The state police are still looking for you two," the oldster said. "You wanta be careful . . ."

"We are," said Johnny, "that's why we're doing things your way. You won some money from me and I've paid it. But we're not going to stand for any more holdups. So give me my car key and we'll be on our way . . ."

The old man started for the back room. "That's fair enough."

Johnny kept close on Johnson's heels, leaving Sam in the filling station with the assistant.

Johnson had a little trouble locating the Chevrolet key. But he found it after a moment on the table; underneath a paper-bound booklet, entitled, *Fifty Simple Card Tricks*.

Johnny scowled when he saw the book. "Card tricks, eh? And your cards, too."

The old man showed his teeth in a wide grin. "I'm only learning, but I got the false shuffle down pretty good. And my one-handed cut ain't bad."

Johnny grabbed him with one hand and with the other reached into his nightshirt. He brought out the bills he had given him a moment ago. The old man howled to high heaven "That's robbery!"

"What do you call what you did to me?"

"Gambling — anything goes in gambling. It says in the book, 'never give a sucker a break!'"

"The sucker's making his own break this time," said Johnny. "Here's thirty bucks for the valve-grinding job — although I doubt if your stooge even ground them."

"I'll get the state police after you," the old man threatened.

"Thanks for reminding me of them," said Johnny. He stepped to the telephone, took hold of the receiver and ripped the cord from the instrument.

"Now you can practice your card tricks, without being interrupted." He stepped into the other room, nodded to Sam. "You drive the station wagon."

They left the filling station with the old proprietor in the doorway shouting dire threats at them. Johnny climbed into the Chevrolet. The motor started with the first touch on the starter button.

He reached over to the glove compartment, opened it and grunted in satisfaction as he took out a book — *Tombstone Days*. He waved to Sam Cragg and rolled the Chevrolet out onto the highway.

He shifted into high and stepped hard on the gas pedal. He gave the little car everything it had for a mile, then began braking.

Sam Cragg pulled up beside him after a moment. "Turn the bus around, heading the other way, then leave it there."

Sam turned the car, then came over to the Chevrolet. "What's the idea of that?"

"Joe Cotter. He's overdue and he knows we left in Henderson's station wagon. I'm hoping he'll think we deserted the bus and started out across the sand . . . Damn! I think that's him now."

Far down the road headlights appeared. Johnny slid over in the seat, indicating that he wanted Sam Cragg to drive. Sam climbed in behind the wheel.

"I thought we were through running from Joe Cotter."

"I need a little time. Step on it."

"Where to?"

"Back to Hansonvllle."

The headlights were growing larger and in a moment flashed past Sam and Johnny, moving at such speed, however, that they could not identify the occupant of the car. But looking back, Johnny saw the tail-lights become redder and knew that the car was stopping for the station wagon.

"Okay," he said, and reached up to switch on the overhead light. Sam exclaimed.

"Don't do that — I can't see as well."

"See as well as you can. I've got to read."

"At a time like this?"

"If I'd had sense enough to read more before, we might never have gotten into this jam," Johnny retorted. "I'm more and more convinced that the solution to this business is right here in this book."

Sam grunted beside him and Johnny opened the book. He turned to the index and found his place. He began reading:

. . . Crime certainly didn't pay for Jim Fargo, but his friend who was enriched by his death, erected a tombstone over his grave that shamed the surviving relatives of more illustrious personages. The tombstone was fully eight feet tall and Hansonville boasted that it was solid silver, dug from the Silver Tombstone mine. This story was given credence for sometime by the fact that an armed guard was posted at the grave. But one night, certain persons got the guard drunk and attacked the tombstone with hammers and chisels. Their reward was a handful of base lead and thereafter the remains of Jim Fargo slumbered in the ground without the tread of a guard overhead . . .

Johnny's eyes jerked up from the book; Sam Cragg was braking the car, preparatory to turning right on the Hansonville road. Johnny saw that full daylight was only a few minutes away.

"Let me know when we get to Hansonville," he said and dropped his eyes once more to the book.

But there was only one more sentence.

Today, Jim Walker is living in his fine mansion near the Silver Tombstone, actively supervising the operations of his famous mine.

Tombstone Days having been published in 1886, the author did not know that the Silver Tombstone went into borrasca within a few months and was abandoned.

Johnny Fletcher closed the book and stared at the road ahead in frowning concentration. The car began slowing up.

"There she is, Johnny!"

Johnny roused himself. "Stop and let me take the wheel."

The exchange of seats was quickly

made and Johnny drove carefully into the hamlet of Hansonville. It was broad daylight, but the village was still asleep.

Once through the town Johnny drove faster and passed the grounds of the Hansonville mine without slowing up. But as he neared the Silver Tombstone he began applying the brakes.

"Johnny!" exclaimed Sam. "We're not going down in the mine again, are we?"

"I hope not," said Johnny grimly as he shut off the engine. He got out of the car, then turned back. "The shotgun, Sam!"

Sam already had it in his hands. He climbed out of the car, scowled as he looked toward the mine shaft.

"Do you see anything of a house around here?" Johnny asked.

Sam looked suspiciously at Johnny. "What kind of a house?"

"A mansion. It says in this book that Jim Walker built a mansion here." He held up the copy.

"If there's a mansion anywhere

around here," said Sam, "it's hiding under a rock."

"Or behind one." Johnny looked at the mound behind the mine shaft. "Let's take a look."

They started for the mine shaft, Sam glanced darkly at the shaft as they passed. Johnny stopped a moment, then, trying to decide whether to climb the mountain of shale and slag, or circle it. He finally determined on the latter course and started toward the left, in the direction away from the Hansonville mine.

It took several minutes to circle the mountain, but before they completed the circuit, Johnny stopped and sniffed the crisp morning air. "Smoke," he announced.

Sam's face set in grim lines. He stepped ahead, the shotgun held at the ready. Fifty feet more and they both saw it — Jim Walker's 'mansion.'

Fifty years is a long time on the desert. Of Jim Walker's old home there remained only the stone walls — and those were buried in the sand to a depth of two or three feet, up to and even above the levels of the glassless windows. Once, no doubt, Walker's house had been a showplace, but now it was a heap of stone and rubble.

In front of what had once been the main door was a small fire and huddled over this was Dan Tompkins, erstwhile desert rat. He was frying bacon in a blackened pan.

He was a little more engrossed in his job than he should have been, for Johnny and Sam were less than twenty yards away before Tompkins became aware of their presence. Then he set down the frying pan and in the same movement reached toward his hip. His hand stopped in mid-air, however, as he saw the muzzle of Sam's shotgun covering him.

"Well, for the lova Geronimo!" he exclaimed loudly. "If it ain't my old pals, Johnny Fletcher and Sam Cragg!"

"Watch him, Sam!" Johnny exclaimed. He dashed past Dan Tompkins and sprang through the doorway. He was just in time to catch Charles Ralston on his knees, trying frantically to open a Boston bag.

Johnny kicked the bag out of his reach. "Outside, chum!"

"Who do you think you're pushing around?" Ralston demanded.

"I wasn't pushing you around," said Johnny. "Not yet. But it's an idea." He raised his foot and kicked Charles Ralston where a man is supposed to be kicked. Ralston went sprawling through the door. Johnny followed.

"So now you two have paired up," he said, when he came outside once more.

Tompkins moistened his lips with the tip of his tongue. "Mr. Ralston sold me a half interest in the Silver Tombstone. He was willing to make me an attractive offer on account of my experience in mining."

"What'd he sell you — a half interest in the Arizona air?"

Ralston began to bluster. "Look here, Fletcher — "

"It's too early in the morning to look," Johnny snapped. "I suggest you and Tompkins start looking . . . somewhere else."

Tompkins shook his head sadly. "That's what I get for bein' decent to you boys."

"Stop it, Tompkins," Johnny cut in impatiently. "That stuff was all around out in Hollywood, but a lot of sand has blown over the desert since then and I haven't got very much time. You gave me a lot of baloney about . . . "

He stopped, his eyes fixed on the ground. There were three tin plates beside the fire. He started to turn and then Joe Cotter came leaping out of the house.

Johnny tried to cry out a warning to Sam Cragg, but Cotter's flailing right hand struck him a terrific blow on the side of the head and Johnny hit the sand so hard that he almost turned a somersault. He was still down when the shotgun boomed.

Johnny scrambled to his knees, then

threw himself flat once more. The shotgun, thrown away by Sam, missed his head by inches. Johnny's face was still in the sand, when he heard the thud of bone and muscle meeting bone and muscle as Sam and Joe Cotter collided.

He heaved up on his hands and saw the two men locked in the long-delayed struggle. He got to his feet and looked quickly to Charles Ralston and Dan Tompkins, both of whom were watching the fighters with expressions of awe.

19

JOE COTTER was perhaps four inches taller than Sam, but weighed only a few pounds more. That he was the strongest man in Arizona, as had been claimed for him, Johnny did not doubt when he saw the terrific strain on Sam Cragg's face. The men, at the moment, were still struggling for grips. As fast as one secured a grip the other broke it.

Sam suddenly broke the deadlock by dropping to his knees and lunging forward. The result was that Cotter went spilling over his shoulder. Sam whirled to throw himself down on Cotter. The big man was too fast, however. His powerful legs doubled, his feet went out and caught Sam Cragg squarely in the midsection.

Sam was hurled backwards for more than a dozen feet. But he was up instantly. So was Joe Cotter. The two men sized each other up, then advanced simultaneously.

This time Cotter decided to slug it out. When he came within range, he feinted with his left, then smashed at Sam with his right. Sam rolled with the blow, taking it high on his shoulder, and came back with a smash that caught Joe Cotter on the chest with the sound of a mallet on a wooden block. Joe Cotter went back a step or two, then braced himself and waited for Sam to come in.

Sam swung with his fist, stopped the punch in mid-air and lunged for Cotter with his head and shoulders. Cotter locked his hands together and as Sam's head hit his torso smashed down with the hands on the back of Sam's neck.

Cotter went down but Sam fell on top of him, groggy from the savage rabbit punch. Cotter struggled to throw Sam off. He finally managed, but Sam's hand snaked out and caught Cotter's ankle. He jerked and Cotter crashed down once more.

Up to now both men had fought reasonably fair. But Cotter, in landing this time, lashed out with his foot and caught Sam squarely in the face with it. Blood gushed from Sam's mouth. He reeled back.

"Goddam you!" he swore.

Cotter bounced to his feet. "Watch yourself from here on," he snarled. "I'm going to beat you to a pulp."

"Come ahead!" Sam challenged. He rushed in, took a terrific blow on his bleeding mouth, but stuck his right hand through Cotter's crotch. His left he wrapped about the bigger man's neck. He lifted Cotter then and hurled him to the ground so hard that Cotter cried out.

Then Sam repeated his mistake of swooping down upon the prostrate Cotter. And again Cotter's feet caught him in the stomach and hurled him back.

Sam was still down this time, when Cotter charged him, kicking savagely.

Sam took a horrible kick in the ribs, tried to roll away, but saw that he couldn't dodge a second kick. His hands therefore shot out and caught Cotter's foot. Cotter, unbalanced, fell beside Sam.

Sam clung to the foot, scrambled aside and came to his feet, still holding Cotter's foot. He began twisting it. Cotter screamed.

"Let go of my foot!"

Viciously he kicked at Sam with his free foot. In a flash Sam had the second foot in his grip. He leaned back then and began turning. Like a hammer thrower throwing a weight, he raised Joe Cotter's body from the sand, made a swift spin and let go.

Cotter flew twenty feet through the air and landed on his head and shoulders. He was still conscious when Sam swooped down, applied the crotch and half Nelson once more, raised him high in the air and slammed him to the earth with every ounce of strength in his body.

Cotter's muscles quivered, but he remained on the ground this time. Sam Cragg turned to Johnny and the others, perspiration and blood streaming from his face.

"Okay, Johnny?" he asked.

"Not bad, Sam. Not bad at all."

A bullet chipped stone from the edge of the door. The sharp crack of a rifle followed immediately. Johnny Fletcher whirled, saw two men descending the mountain of shale. He made a flying jump for the shotgun Sam had thrown away when tackling Joe Cotter. He got his hands on it just as sand was kicked up a few inches away by a second bullet.

He made for the doorway of Old Jim Walker's house, but was delayed for one desperate moment by Dan Tompkins, who in turn was trying to squeeze past both Sam and Charles Ralston.

A rifle cracked a third time and the jam at the door was broken by sheer force at the cost of a little skin.

Then all four men were inside the living room of the ruined mansion and Johnny was whirling back toward the window aperture nearby.

He risked a quick glance out and a bullet fanned his cheek. Swearing roundly, Johnny poked out the shotgun muzzle and pulled the trigger. There were yells of pain outside. Johnny looked out and saw both Danny Sage and Mike Henderson scrambling back up the slope of shale, out of range of the shotgun.

Johnny ducked under the window ledge, turned to Charles Ralston. "Where's that pop gun you were looking for awhile ago?"

Charles Ralston dropped to his knees beside his bag. He tore it open and searched frantically for his gun. After a moment he turned. "Here . . . !"

Johnny groaned when he saw the tiny .32 caliber pistol. "I thought you had a gun." Nevertheless, he took it.

Sam exclaimed, "What's the matter

with the shotgun?"

"It's a double-barreled gun. You fired one shell and I just fired the other. I only hope they don't know we haven't any more shells for it."

A bullet ricocheted off the windowsill and smashed into the wall beyond. Johnny took a quick peek outside, saw that both Henderson and Sage had halted on the slope, about halfway up. They were about a hundred yards away, beyond shotgun — and .32 caliber pistol-range.

The two men began firing methodically now, sending bullets through the open doorway and window. Ralston, Tompkins, Sam and Johnny either dropped flat or remained on their knees, directly under the window.

A moment or two passed before Johnny remembered that Tompkins had reached for his hip when he and Sam had come up. "What's the matter with *your* rod?" he asked.

Tompkins swallowed hard. "I been using it for bluff. Uh, the firing pin's been broke two-three months now."

The shooting outside stopped. "Come on out!" yelled the voice of Danny Sage. "You haven't got a chance."

Johnny raised his head to look out of the window. "Go to hell!"

The answer to that was a bullet through the window and after a moment, another. There was a pause of about a half minute, then a third bullet came through.

Johnny exclaimed, "That's the same gun shooting." He crawled suddenly on his hands and knees to the door, glanced out quickly.

"Henderson's out there alone!" he cried "Danny Sage is sneaking around to the rear . . . Wait here . . . !"

He scuttled across the floor to an open doorway leading back into the house. Safe in a hallway, covered with a foot of sand, he came to his feet and started running through the rooms.

There were quite a few of them, for Walker's mansion had been a large one, but as the doors were all off their hinges it was a job of straight running and he negotiated the distance in quick time.

When he burst out of the rear door he was just in time to see Danny Sage coming around the corner. He thrust out the revolver and sent two quick snap shots at the Indian. Danny turned and ran back the way he had come.

Johnny hesitated, wondering if he should go back to the front of the house. The situation was impossible. He couldn't keep running from the front to the rear and then back again. Sooner or later Sage and Henderson would guess that there was only one gun in the entire house — a gun with four remaining cartridges.

Sam Cragg came padding up behind Johnny, and decided Johnny upon his course of action.

"Come on," he said in a low tone to Sam, "we'll let them hold the fort."

"Without a gun?"

"Without a gun!" retorted Johnny.

"None of this is our fight in the first place."

He started off, across the sand in the general direction of a heap of rocks and boulders a hundred yards or so behind the house. He bent low, running swiftly and Sam Cragg pounded behind him.

They were within a few feet of the first boulders when a bullet kicked up gravel ahead of Johnny. He whirled, and swore. He had forgotten the eminence in front of the house. From the top of it Mike Henderson could see clear across the ruins. And he could shoot across the house, too . . . A range of about three hundred yards, not too much for a good rifleman.

Johnny dove for the shelter of the boulders. A bullet took off Sam's right heel and he cried out as he tripped and fell headlong. But he scrambled up quickly and came to take shelter behind the oblong rock where Johnny was already sprawled.

"Here we go again," Johnny snarled,

"acting as clay pigeons."

A bullet whacked into the stone above Johnny's head with a dull *thuck*!

Johnny rolled over on his side, looked up. "The tombstone!" he exclaimed.

"Huh?"

"Jim Fargo's." Johnny reached up. "Look — the inscription . . . '*Jim Fargo, Died here, July 18, 1883. He was a loyal friend.*'"

"Let's get away from here," Sam Cragg said uneasily. "You know I don't like graves, and besides, this one's caved in."

"What?" Johnny fixed his eyes on the depression behind Sam. Then he turned carefully, crawled forward two or three feet, then down into a hole.

"Nix, Johnny!" Sam complained behind Johnny.

Johnny reached back with the pistol. "Take this," he said over his shoulder.

Sam took the gun and Johnny lowered himself head first down into the hole, until only his heels remained above ground. Then suddenly he began thrashing his legs and Sam, whirling, reached out and caught Johnny's heels.

"Pull me up!" came Johnny's smothered voice.

Sam braced himself in the loose sand and heaved. A bullet kicked up sand only a couple of feet away, but Sam persisted and slowly tugged Johnny out of the hole.

Johnny crawled back behind the shelter of the tombstone. He was seething with excitement. "That wasn't any cave-in, Sam!" he exclaimed. "It was dug."

"Who'd dig into an old grave?"

"Tompkins," said Johnny promptly. "There's solid rock five feet under this sand."

"So what?"

"The answer's in the book over in the car. I had just about guessed it anyway, but this is a dead giveaway. It's the reason for . . ."

He broke off and raised his head suddenly.

Sam heard it too. "A police siren!" he gasped.

"The cops!"

It was a siren, all right, And it was near, on the road just a few hundred yards away. It rose in pitch, then began dying out in a long wail.

Johnny looked around the tombstone, saw both Mike Henderson and Danny Sage climbing to the top of the slag mountain. For a moment they stood on the very crest, their rifles raised high. Then they threw down their weapons.

Johnny got to his feet. "The state police stopped in at the filling station."

"I guess we never had a chance," Sam said, wearily.

"What do you mean?"

"We go to jail, don't we?"

"What for? The case is solved, isn't it?"

"What case?"

"The murder of Hugh Kitchen — naturally. What else have the cops got against us?"

306

Sam blinked. "I don't know — what have they?"

"Not a thing!" Then he winced. "Except that bill at the filling station."

"All right, you men . . . " yelled a loud voice. "Come on in!"

20

A UNIFORMED state trooper appeared in the rear door of Jim Walker's house. He was holding a very efficient-looking tommy gun. Johnny dropped Charles Ralston's little pistol and started forward. Before he reached the house, however, people began pouring out . . . Laura Henderson, Helen Walker, Charles Ralston, Dan Tompkins, Mike Henderson and Danny Sage. And finally a very wobbly Joe Cotter. He was followed by a second trooper, with a machine gun.

"You're all under arrest," announced the first state trooper, as Johnny and Sam approached.

"What's the charge?" Johnny asked briskly.

"We'll figure them out later." The trooper pointed the tommy gun at Johnny. "That Chevvy with the

California plates . . . it belongs to you?"

"Me and the finance company."

"All right, then, that's the first complaint. You owe a little bill . . . "

"To Johnson," Johnny said promptly. "One hundred bucks. I paid him for grinding the valves. Here's the money." He brought out a roll of bills from his pocket. "This is a lot of money to pay for a couple of card tricks."

"Card tricks!" exclaimed the trooper. "What do you mean?"

"He's got a book — *Fifty Simple Card Tricks*." As the trooper reddened, "You haven't been playing gin rummy with him, have you?"

"No," said the trooper. "Of course not, but wait'll I see that old goat!"

Johnny chuckled.

The second trooper came forward. "That doesn't explain all this shooting that's been going on here."

"No," said Johnny, "that's another matter. Murder . . . "

"Look here, officers," Mike Henderson

cut in, "this man is wanted for murder in California . . . "

"Not me," retorted Johnny.

"His name's Fletcher!" cried Henderson. "There was an alarm out for him . . . "

"Johnny Fletcher?" exclaimed the first state trooper.

"Yes! He killed a man named Hugh Kitchen . . . "

Two tommy guns were suddenly trained on Johnny. Johnny held up his right hand and pointed at Dan Tompkins. "Tompkins, what did you find under Jim Fargo's grave?"

Dan Tompkins winced. "Whaddya mean?"

"I fell into the hole."

"I don't know what you're talking about."

"I've got a book in my car," said Johnny. "It's called *Tombstone Days* and there's quite a lot in it about how Jim Walker found the Silver Tombstone mine when he went to bury his friend, Jim Fargo . . . "

"Everybody knows that story," said Tompkins. "But Walker didn't bury Fargo where he intended to bury him. That's over there . . . " He waved toward the slag mountain. "Where Walker dug his shaft."

Johnny nodded. "I know — he struck a rich vein there. So he buried his friend back here." He pointed to the tombstone over the grave. "And for quite awhile he had an armed guard watching over the grave. Why do you suppose he did that?"

Danny Sage said quietly: "There was a rumor that the tombstone was made of solid silver. But it wasn't. I was talking to my great-uncle, Bill Sage, only last night. He says the tombstone's lead."

"I guess it is — but then why did he have a guard watching over it?"

"Because he was crazy!" burst out Mike Henderson.

Laura Henderson exclaimed, "Oh, give it up, Mike. He knows."

"Yes," said Johnny. "I know. I know

that in digging the *second* grave for Jim Fargo, Jim Walker struck a second rich vein of ore . . . a vein that he didn't intend to work at the time. Isn't that right, Miss Walker?" Johnny turned suddenly to Helen Walker.

Helen's face was creased in heavy thought. "I don't know. Uncle Jim used to talk about there being more silver in the Silver Tombstone than he had ever taken out of it, but he was over seventy when he lost his money, and . . . " She looked at Charles Ralston. " . . . and he said that he was going to leave the mine to me so that *I* would be rich."

"He lost his mind after he lost his money!" exclaimed Charles Ralston. "His will was . . . "

"Fight that out in court," Johnny cut in.

"Let's fight *this* out at headquarters," said one of the state troopers.

Joe Cotter shuffled forward. His face was puffed and bruised. "Look, fellows," he said to the troopers, "this is my bailiwick. The least you can do is let me get in my two cents' worth. This bird," pointing at Tompkins, "came to me a few weeks ago and wanted me to dicker for the Silver Tombstone mine. He took me down and showed me a vein of medium grade ore. I didn't think he could make much out of it, but he was willing to pay me for my work. That's how I got mixed in this business myself . . . Then the first thing you know, a lawyer named Hugh Kitchen is murdered over in San Bernardino, California . . . "

"*My* lawyer," Charles Ralston offered.

Cotter nodded. "I never could figure out why *your* lawyer should be knocked off."

"Maybe," suggested Johnny, "it was because he discovered that something was wrong with Jim Walker's will."

He looked at Helen Walker. She was staring at him, her eyes wide, her nostrils flaring.

"That's what I've been telling you all the time," exclaimed Charles Ralston.

"The old boy was out of his mind. They even had him committed to an institution for awhile."

Johnny looked sharply at Helen Walker. "Is that true?"

Helen Walker made no reply. But she shifted her gaze from Johnny Fletcher to Mike Henderson. The young owner of the Hansonville Mining Corporation bit his lower lip with his teeth.

Then suddenly he laughed. "Well, I guess the jig's up. I made my play and — "

He sprang for the nearest state trooper and got hold of the tommy gun with both hands. But the trooper was a game lad. He clung to the gun with all he had. Until Mike Henderson brought his knee up into the trooper's groin. The trooper cried out and fell to the sand. Mike Henderson wrenched the tommy gun free . . . and then the second trooper let him have a burst from his own gun.

★ ★ ★

314

Charles Ralston was just helping Laura Henderson out of Mike's station wagon, when Johnny and Sam drove up to the Hansonville mine in the Chevrolet. Johnny got out of the car and walked over to the others.

"Well, I guess the Silver Tombstone's yours now, Ralston," Johnny said. "Helen Walker's going to be . . . " He stopped, looking at Laura Henderson

"You might as well finish it, Johnny," said Laura Henderson. "Let's get it all out, because after today I'm never going to talk about my brother again."

"He was in borrasca, wasn't he?" Johnny asked.

Laura nodded. "The mine hadn't shown a profit in almost a year. He was always interested in the Silver Tombstone and talked a lot about it — to old men who had been here during the boom days. And he read everything he could about it. Then two weeks ago, he dug into Jim Fargo's grave and discovered its secret. He wrote to Helen Walker and learned that

Dan Tompkins was already dickering with her for the mine . . . and that she was in fact about to drive out here. He wired her to meet him in San Bernardino. I wasn't in San Bernardino myself . . . "

"Why not?" Johnny asked.

"I was supposed to, well, talk to . . . " Laura hesitated. " . . . to Charles."

Ralston looked at her curiously. "To pump me? But I didn't know anything. It was Kitchen . . . "

" . . . Who stopped off in San Bernardino," Johnny finished for Ralston. "And he convinced Helen that Jim Walker's will didn't have a chance in a court, because it had been made just prior to the time that Helen and her mother had had old Jim committed to an institution."

Laura's eyes squinted in pain.

"*She* says Mike did it."

"That's going to be her defense. Although it won't actually make any difference. If Mike did it, she's an accessory and if Mike helped her cover up — by carrying the body out to my car, then *he* was an accessory."

"I know," said Laura miserably.

Johnny looked steadily at Ralston. "Ralston," he said, "did you ever hear of the apex laws?"

"Why, yes," replied Ralston, "I've been reading up on mines. But I don't see . . . "

"The Silver Tombstone adjoins the Hansonville mine. You're bound to get into an argument with each other sooner or later . . . "

"I don't see why we should," Ralston said stiffly.

"The best solution," said Johnny, "is to merge the two mines."

Ralston frowned. "But the Hansonville mine's in borrasca and the Silver Tombstone . . . "

" . . . is in bonanza. But what's the difference . . . if you have them both in the family?"

Ralston suddenly looked at Laura Henderson with a new light in his eyes. Johnny grinned crookedly and walked over to the Chevrolet. He climbed in beside Sam.

"New York, Sam!"

"New York!" cried Sam.

THE END

THE MONTMARTRE MURDERS
Richard Grayson

Inspector Gautier of Sûreté investigates the disappearance of artist Théo, the heir to a fortune.

GRIZZLY TRAIL
Gwen Moffat

Miss Pink, alone in the Rockies, helps in a search for missing hikers, solves two cruel murders and has the most terrifying experience of her life when she meets a grizzly bear!

BLINDMAN'S BLUFF
Margaret Carr

Kate Deverill had considered suicide. It was one way out — and preferable to being murdered.

LITTLE DROPS OF BLOOD
Bill Knox

It might have been just another unfortunate road accident but a few little drops of blood pointed to murder.

GOSSIP TO THE GRAVE
Jonathan Burke

Jenny Clark invented Simon Sherborne because her daily gossip column was getting dull. Then Simon appeared at a party — in the flesh! And Jenny finds herself involved in murder.

HARRIET FAREWELL
Margaret Erskine

Wealthy Theodore Buckler had planned a magnificent Guy Fawkes Day celebration. He hadn't planned on murder.

BEGOTTEN MURDER
Martin Carroll

When Susan Phillips joined her aunt on a voyage of 12,000 miles from her home in Melbourne, she little knew their arrival would germinate the seeds of murder planted long ago.

WHO'S THE TARGET?
Margaret Carr

Three people whom Abby could identify as her parents' murderers wanted her dead, but she decided that maybe Jason could have been the target.

THE LOOSE SCREW
Gerald Hammond

After a motor smash, Beau Pepys and his cousin Jacqueline, her fiancé and dotty mother, suspect that someone had prearranged the death of their friend. But who, and why?

MUD IN HIS EYE
Gerald Hammond

The harbourmaster's body is found mangled beneath Major Smyle's yacht. What is the sinister significance of the illicit oysters?

THE SCAVENGERS
Bill Knox

Among the masses of struggling fish in the *Tecta*'s nets was a larger, darker, ominously motionless form . . . the body of a skin diver.

DEATH IN ARCADY
Stella Phillips

Detective Inspector Matthew Furnival works unofficially with the local police when a brutal murder takes place in a caravan camp.

THE DRACULA MURDERS
Philip Daniels

The Horror Ball was interrupted by a spectral figure who warned the merrymakers they were tampering with the unknown.

THE LADIES
OF LAMBTON GREEN
Liza Shepherd

Why did murdered Robin Colquhoun's picture pose such a threat to the ladies of Lambton Green?

CARNABY
AND THE GAOLBREAKERS
Peter N. Walker

Detective Sergeant James Aloysius Carnaby-King is sent to prison as bait. When he joins in an escape he is thrown headfirst into a vicious murder hunt.

A FOOT IN THE GRAVE
Bruce Marshall

About to be imprisoned and tortured in Buenos Aires, John Smith escapes, only to become involved in an aeroplane hijacking.

DEAD TROUBLE
Martin Carroll

Trespassing brought Jennifer Denning more than she bargained for. She was totally unprepared for the violence which was to lie in her path.

HOURS TO KILL
Ursula Curtiss

Margaret went to New Mexico to look after her sick sister's rented house and felt a sharp edge of fear when the absent landlady arrived.

MURDER TO BURN
Laurie Mantell

Sergeants Steven Arrow and Lance Brendon, of the New Zealand police force, come upon a woman's body in the water. When the dead woman is identified they begin to realise that they are investigating a complex fraud.

YOU CAN HELP ME
Maisie Birmingham

Whilst running the Citizens' Advice Bureau, Kate Weatherley is attacked with no apparent motive. Then the body of one of her clients is found in her room.

DAGGERS DRAWN
Margaret Carr

Stacey Manston was the kind of girl who could take most things in her stride, but three murders were something different . . .

STORM CENTRE
Douglas Clark

Detective Chief Superintendent Masters, temporarily lecturing in a police staff college, finds there's more to the job than a few weeks relaxation in a rural setting.

THE MANUSCRIPT MURDERS
Roy Harley Lewis

Antiquarian bookseller Matthew Coll, acquires a rare 16th century manuscript. But when the Dutch professor who had discovered the journal is murdered, Coll begins to doubt its authenticity.

SHARENDEL
Margaret Carr

Ruth didn't want all that money. And she didn't want Aunt Cass to die. But at Sharendel things looked different. She began to wonder if she had a split personality.

THE DEATH OF ABBE DIDIER
Richard Grayson

Inspector Gautier of the Sûreté investigates three crimes which are strangely connected.

NIGHTMARE TIME
Hugh Pentecost

Have the missing major and his wife met with foul play somewhere in the Beaumont Hotel, or is their disappearance a carefully planned step in an act of treason?

BLOOD WILL OUT
Margaret Carr

Why was the manor house so oddly familiar to Elinor Howard? Who would have guessed that a Sunday School outing could lead to murder?